BOOKS BY MARK SCHORER

———————————

A House Too Old (1935)

The Hermit Place (1941)

William Blake: The Politics of Vision (1946)

The State of Mind: Thirty-Two Stories (1947)

The Story: A Critical Anthology (1950)

The Wars of Love (1954)

Sinclair Lewis: An American Life (1961)

D. H. Lawrence (1968)

The World We Imagine: Selected Essays (1968)

The Literature of America: Twentieth Century (1970)

Pieces of Life (1977)

PIECES OF LIFE

MARK SCHORER

PIECES OF LIFE

FARRAR, STRAUS AND GIROUX

NEW YORK

FOR RUTH HART

CONTENTS

AUTHOR'S NOTE

The stories in this volume which have been previously published are as follows: "Is Anything Troubling You, Dear?," "Of Educational Value," "The Face within the Face," "Picking Up the Pieces," and "The Lonely Constellation," all in *The New Yorker;* "Another Country" in *Esquire;* "A Burning Garden" in *Botteghe Oscure XX;* "Don't Take Me for Granted" in *Rogue;* and "A Lamp" in *The Atlantic Monthly.* All these stories appear here in the order of their publication, which is also that of their composition. "The Unwritten Story" at the end, which appears here for the first time, is also the most recent.

As for the autobiographical interstices, unpublished until now, I can only say that I wanted the characters in the stories to act out their problems before a darker backdrop than the stories themselves provide, nothing lugubrious, nothing narcissistic certainly, nothing self-pitying, I trust, but yet something more shadowy, bleaker, than what goes on downstage. These fragments of autobiography, mostly about my early years, can probably not be read as counterpoint to the stories, since thematic relationships are, as far as I can see, almost nonexistent. (I may be deceived.) But I hope that they provide a loosely linked coherence, the marching rhythm of another but accompanying drum, the slightly staggering dissonance of a real life beating beneath the surface of brighter, created lives.

'Twill soon be dark;

Up! mind thine own aim, and

God speed the mark!

EMERSON

PIECES OF LIFE

VILLAGE

The town in which I was brought up, Sauk City, had been there, on that curve of the Wisconsin River, for only sixty-seven years when I was born. Not until now, making an effort to summon up my earliest recollections, do I see how near the frontier we still were. Although the site was discovered and the village platted in 1841 by a Hungarian adventurer-aristocrat, Count Augoston Haraszthy (later to develop a Sonoma, California, vineyard, still in operation), most of the early settlers were Germans who left their homeland in that troubled revolutionary decade. In my early years, German was still the common language in the village. Among those early settlers was a group of relatively literate atheists who organized themselves under the name *Frei-Gemeinde* and on the walls of whose meeting place, along with large framed portrait engravings of such worthies as Goethe, Schiller, and Beethoven, hung one of Karl Marx. There was also a Roman Catholic church and an Evangelical Reformed church (Lutheran, in effect) to which my family belonged. Church services in my childhood were conducted in German but the Sunday-school classes were conducted in English. The family of my mother's mother, Grandma Jaeger, was among that group of early German immigrants.

Photographs of the main street (Water Street, because it ran alongside and above the river) taken in the first decade of this century bear out my own first recollections: a rather broad, often muddy, rutted road, wooden sidewalks, straggling buildings most of which (including my grandmother's little variety store—"notions") boasted rectangular false fronts, both sides of the street lined with hitching railings for horses. On Saturday nights, when the farmers from the outlying areas came to town for their weekly marketing, the street was crowded with their wagons, their horses tied up to these railings. When the weather permitted, all the inhabitants of the village would also be "down town," as the street was known, on Saturday nights, shopping, gossiping, mothers with infants in arms or pulling small children along by the hand on the rough boardwalks. By then the population of the place had grown to about eight hundred.

IS ANYTHING TROUBLING YOU, DEAR?

Mr. Farnham was talking on the phone in the bedroom when he heard the elevator door close in the hallway outside the apartment. "I'll meet you," he said. "Don't call back." He hastily put the phone down and walked through the living room and into the foyer just as his wife came in.

"Hello," she said. "Home already?"

"It's past six," he answered.

They went into the living room together. "I know," she said. "I'm sorry, but I've been with Helen Chivvey and I couldn't get away. You know Helen Chivvey!"

"Helen Chivvey?" Mr. Farnham said vaguely.

"We used to see the Chivveys now and then. They've been in Washington since 1942. Now they're back. Helen's a great talker! She's Stratton '23, too."

"Oh," said Mr. Farnham. "The Fund."

"Yes." Mrs. Farnham lit several lamps and then sat down heavily in a large chintz-covered chair. "Get me a sherry, Ralph," she said, and pulled off her gloves. She struggled out of the sleeves of her coat and let it slip down behind her shoulders, and then lifted her veil away from her face but did not take off her hat. She opened the large bag in her lap, looked through a pack of subscription cards, which were headed Stratton College Mother-Daughter Scholarship Fund, and studied some names and neatly written sums in a small red leather notebook. She heard the telephone ring and was vaguely aware of Ralph's voice saying quietly, "Yes . . . No, I didn't . . . No . . . No . . . Yes . . . As soon as I can," but she was intent on her statistics, and when Ralph came back from the buffet in the dining room with a sherry for her and a short high-ball, she said, without looking up, "Ralph, I'm really doing very well. Much better than I had hoped."

"Good," he said. He put her sherry on the round mahogany table beside her chair and hovered there, as if he wanted to speak.

She was still studying her notebook and asked abstractedly, "Who telephoned?"

He said, "The office. I've got to go back down tonight." He walked to the other side of the hearth and sat down facing her in another large chintz-covered chair.

Mrs. Farnham looked up. "How irritating! I wanted you to take me to that French movie about the Maquis. It's supposed to be very good."

"We have a big client in town. Very important. He's leaving later tonight and we have to settle some things before he goes." He took a long drink of his highball and nearly emptied the glass. "We're having some food sent up to the office."

"You can't even have dinner? Oh, Ralph!"

"Can't be helped."

"Well, I *am* tired. I guess I'll have my dinner on a tray right here and then go to bed. This campaign is exhausting me. Women like Helen Chivvey—"

"Why do you do it? How do you keep up your interest in Stratton anyway? Not to mention all the other worthy causes."

"There are two kinds of alumnae, Ralph, and believe me, when you're involved in this kind of soliciting, you learn to tell them apart. There are the responsible women and the irresponsible." She sipped her sherry contentedly.

Mr. Farnham finished his drink and stood up. "I guess I'd better get along," he said.

"Wait a minute. I want to tell you about the Chiveys. It's a fantastic story. Have another drink."

Mr. Farnham looked at the pink china clock on the white mantel. "Well, a quick one," he said, and went into the dining room.

Mrs. Farnham stood up with a sigh and laid her coat over the arm of a sofa. Then she took one of the long matches for the fireplace from its flowered container and lit the fire. She was a rather stout woman, and when she bent over the grate the black material of her dress stretched tautly over her heavy hips. She straightened up, her face flushed, and pulled at her girdle. Then she sat down in the same chair, her gloves and the bag shoved down beside her on the seat, and sipped her sherry. She heard Ralph in the dining room and she began to speak to him in a loud voice.

"When they came back from Washington, they had a hard time finding a place to live, of course. Nothing in town at all. But, finally, Helen found this house in Riverdale. It's a pretty, old house, but like everything now, there's a catch to it. They have to live with this old blind man."

"Blind man?" Mr. Farnham asked as he came back in. He filled her glass from the decanter he carried and put it on the table beside the glass. Then he sat down in the chair facing her.

"Yes, blind. He's the owner of the house, and he's old,

and he's all alone in the world, and of course he *needs* tenants—to help him out, sort of. I suppose the housing shortage is really a lifesaver for him. He keeps one room at the head of the stairs, and he has a bath, and the tenants take care of his room and give him his breakfast up there and help him when he's at a loss for anything. Of course, he's lived there for years, and knows the house, and he always goes to the same restaurant for his meals, and he seems to get along very well. I saw him."

"You did?" Mr. Farnham did not seem quite to be listening.

"It's pathetic, Ralph, it really is. Of course, if you don't remember Helen Chivvey, half the point is lost."

Mr. Farnham's gray eyes were focused vacantly on a point on the wall behind her and his thin face looked vaguely troubled. Mrs. Farnham did not notice, and the fire crackled comfortably between them.

"Helen never stops talking. I remember in college, girls who didn't like her used to say she had some kind of nervous disease which kept her talking all the time. There was a name for it."

"Does she still have it?" Mr. Farnham asked, as his troubled gaze came down from the wall to his wife's plump, cheerful face.

Mrs. Farnham laughed impatiently. "Nervous disease! She's just terribly self-engrossed. Everything pertaining to herself has importance out of all reasonable proportion. I could hardly stop her long enough to explain the idea of the Mother-Daughter Scholarship Fund. Of course, she did pledge a hundred and fifty dollars, but then, the motives for charity are so mixed . . . It certainly doesn't prove that she's really generous, or even interested in Stratton. And by the way, Ralph, I'll probably have to go up there next week."

"So? What about the blind man?"

"Why, simply this. Here is Helen, all wrapped up in herself and her husband and her children. Nothing else. I don't know if I can explain it, Ralph, but it struck me as really dreadful. For instance, I told her that I was the New York chairman of the Fund and that Katherine was the senior chairman on the campus, and that we thought that was rather cute, and so on. Did she ask a word about Katherine? Not one. She began immediately to tell me a long saga about *her* daughter, who, it seems, left college for a commission in the lady Marines, and all about her experiences, and from that to her son, who was at Los Alamos, and since we were on the war, I began to tell her a little about my work as a volunteer nurse, but then she switched off to social life in Washington during the war. She's so *boring*, that's all! All self-centered people really are, I've decided. I finally brought her down to the subject of the Fund by simply interrupting and saying, 'Look, Helen—'"

Mr. Farnham was nervously smoking a cigarette. He had finished his drink, and he leaped up suddenly. "What about the blind man? I ought to go."

"She told me all about him—how helpless and how tiresome he is, and how he wants conversation, their company, and how they pretend to be *out* when they're in! The living room of their house opens off the hallway you enter, and the stairs go up just across from the living-room door, and Helen always puts the old man's mail on the newel post for him. And just as she was telling me all this, we heard slow steps on the porch, and the sound of a cane tapping, and Helen said, 'Now be absolutely quiet!' Then the old man came in. He felt for his mail on the newel post, but there was none, and then he turned toward the living room, where we were sitting in plain sight—I mean, of course, anyone else's sight—and turned his head slowly from side to side, as though he were looking up and down the length of the room. His eyes are open, and, Ralph, they *look* all right! That's what's so alarming. The old man said, 'Mrs. Chivvey, did I hear you?' in the most appalling way, and Helen put her finger on her lips quickly, and we both sat motionless, and I found myself even holding my breath. Then he went slowly up the stairs to his room, and after we heard his door close, Helen rolled her eyes and said softly, '*That's* the way we have to live!' "

Mr. Farnham said, "Ugh—sordid! Still, the old fellow is probably a bore."

"But that's the point, Ralph. He couldn't possibly be as boring as Helen. And there she sits, really more blind to everything but herself than he is, *pretending* to see, to be so superior, when she's— Well, thank heavens I've checked her off my list! Tomorrow I'm lunching with Jane Garvin and in the afternoon I'm seeing Pudge Linton and Harriet Bender. They're all all right."

Mr. Farnham said, "Well, I've got to go, dear," but after he spoke, he seemed to hesitate.

Mrs. Farnham said, "Oh, Ralph, advise me! I had a letter this morning asking if I'd consider becoming a candidate for office in the League of Women Voters—the national office. What do you think? This last thing has tired me so I just feel like taking a rest."

The telephone rang again and Mr. Farnham went rapidly into the bedroom to answer it. This time Mrs. Farnham listened, and a woman spoke so harshly and imperiously—or so it seemed—into the wire that the sound of her voice carried clearly into the living room. Mrs. Farnham heard Ralph answer softly, saying, "Yes . . . Yes . . . Yes," and "Right away."

When he came back into the living room, he had his hat on and his topcoat over his arm.

"Goodness!" Mrs. Farnham said. "Who was that? Such an unpleasant voice!"

He laughed uneasily. "Oh, Roger's secretary. Her

voice is unfortunate, but she's really very good at her job. I'm late and have to go."

"But she sounded as though she were giving you orders!"

"Oh, no. That's just her voice."

Then Mr. Farnham still hesitated, and he looked at his wife as if he wished to tell her something more but did not know how to begin. She pulled her bag out from beside her and opened it again, and she began to shuffle through the pages of the notebook. His eyes took on a helpless stare as he watched her, and presently, when she became aware that he was still standing in front of her, she looked up and said, "Aren't you going?"

"Oh, yes, yes. Goodbye, dear."

"Goodbye, Ralph." Then when he was nearly at the door, she called, "Ralph, you aren't troubled about anything, are you?"

"No, not at all. Why?"

"You looked so strange just then."

He laughed weakly and walked out, and before she went back to her names and figures, Mrs. Farnham, her hat still on, sat for a few moments with her head cocked, listening to him bring up the elevator, step into it, close the door behind him, and go down.

HOUSEHOLD

If my father had had even five hundred dollars when, in 1905, he married my mother, why hadn't he tried to work out other housekeeping arrangements? Was it, conceivably, simply assumed, in that kind of hinterland community, that a young groom moved into the house of his bride's mother and, as it happened in this instance, her stepfather? And this after his melodramatic threat of withdrawal? Or were these matters possibly interwoven, the threat of withdrawal countered by the promise of a considerable house of his own as soon as possible, in the meantime the upper floor of this house available, and the marriage hastily brought to a head, the suspense over for the bride and her mother? And even for the rough stepfather? In a flurry of some sort of scandal, my grandmother had divorced my mother's father, or had been divorced by him; it was the first divorce in that community. Conrad Jaeger, the stepfather, must himself have been an uneasy outsider, an experienced older counterpart to the good-looking, dark,

choir-singing young newcomer to the town, that rigid innocent, my father.

Whatever the circumstances, it was in that house that
my older brother (1906) and I (1908) were born. The upper floor was ours: three small rooms, in the smallest of
which my father, about fifty years before pop art, had pa-
pered one wall with pea can labels and which was, insofar
as there was any, their sitting room. There was, of course,
no running water but, instead, little-used commodes in the
bedrooms, much-used slop jars, a hand pump in the kitchen
sink below, and a pump over the well outside at the foot of
the steps off the kitchen porch. There was, of course, no
central heating, only a wood-burning range in the kitchen
and a coal stove (rather tall, bellied, isinglass-covered squares
in its door) in the sitting room. That room was immediately
off the kitchen, and there, under a light fixture that could
be lifted or lowered (a kerosene lamp), was a round table
that could be extended to seat ten people (if all other furniture was pushed aside) when there was some occasion for
not eating, as we normally did, in the kitchen.

Off the sitting room were two rooms: one was the bedroom of the grandparents, beyond a double door opening
hung with heavily fringed portieres; the other, beyond always closed double doors, was the "parlor," mysterious as a
seldom-glimpsed shrine, and never, in my recollections from
my time in that house, used as a living room.

It was in 1912 or 1913 that we moved from that house
into what my grandparents had built for my parents as our
own. My grandparents were, in their own lives, quite mi-
serly, and were thought to have a fortune. Our house, for
that time and place, was rather splendid—nine rooms, interior plumbing, central heating, electricity—everything that
they denied themselves. When they died in the 1930's, their
estate proved to be respectable but hardly lavish. I remember parental disappointment.

OF

EDUCATIONAL

VALUE

"Frustration! Frustration!" Professor Miles heard his wife exclaim as she came into the entry hall. Her tone was animated and cheerful; she might almost as well have called, "All in the day's work!" or "Hello! Hello!" He listened to her fasten the night latch, and then she did call, "Hello? Gilbert? Hello?"

Her clear, clipped voice came to him through the empty living room into his small library, where he sat by the fire. He looked up from the pages of the first volume of Lecky on England in the eighteenth century (he had been reading about the baiting of animals and the general depravity of middle-class taste) and called back, "I'm in here." The expression on his narrow white face changed from interested studiousness to a kind of watchful, bright-eyed intentness. She was rattling coat hangers on the rod in the hall closet. Briskly, neat heels tapping on the waxed floor, she then came across the living room, but when she appeared in the doorway of the library, her small, damp, and bedraggled look was in sharp contrast to the efficient sounds that had preceded her. It was only then that Gilbert Miles became aware of the real storm outside; the wind was blowing rain against the windows in gusty sheets.

"Frustration! Absolute frustration!" Marian Miles said with amiable force. She had a little black felt hat in her hand—a very wet hat—and she shook it out as she advanced to the fire.

"Get wet?"

"That's the least of it." She sat d   n an uphol-stered stool before the fireplace and balanced the hat on the fender. Then she took off her shoes. Because she was quite short, she always wore high heels and these shoes consisted of little more than high heels, soles, and pockets for the toes. The nylon-covered feet that they had con-tained were dark with wetness. "The very least of it," she said as she lifted one of her pretty legs and peeled off a stocking. "Such a fiasco!" she continued as she peeled off the other. She draped the wet stockings over the fender, beside her hat, and wriggled her damp toes before the fire.

"Where were you?" Gilbert asked. "Red Cross?"

"I told you at dinner where I was going."

"Civic League?"

"No! P.T.A.!" she said with good-humored exaspera-tion.

"Oh, yes."

"I am the Program Committee." She laughed, with that note of self-depreciation that he had often affection-ately observed as remarkable, because it was almost totally innocent of self-perception.

"Oh, yes."

"Do you remember now?"

He smiled fleetingly. "Well . . ."

She bent toward the fire and shook out her damp short hair. "Very well, I'll tell it all to you again, *plus!*" she said.

He glanced down at his book and said hastily, "It says here that in a certain popular entertainment in which the people killed a cock by throwing sharp sticks at him the bird was supposed to symbolize France—the English antipathy, you know."

"No, you don't!" she exclaimed. "You'll hear me out. You call me Mrs. Do-Good, and you won't ever help me, but at least you can listen to me."

Professor Miles put a slim ivory paper cutter in his book, closed it, and laid it on the table beside his chair. "You are the Program Committee . . ." he said.

"And I was determined that this year the programs would make some sense," Marian said. "Have some educational value. I proposed Music of All Peoples, one People for every meeting, different women to handle different People. And because it was such a touchy subject, I chose for myself Music of the Negro."

"African chants?" Professor Miles asked with impassive malice.

"Music of the *American* Negro."

"Oh. That would be jazz?"

"No, Gilbert! Spirituals. But authentic, you know. And so I had arranged with that young Negress, that Burkman girl—Editha Burkman, you know; we heard her sing at the Wallace rally; she's very good—I had arranged with her to come to the meeting tonight to sing spirituals. I was to get her. But I did the silliest thing, Gilbert. I called her Miss Black!"

He moved forward, with a slight, startled jerk of the head. "You called her Miss Black, dear? Why did you do that?"

She shook her head impatiently. "I don't know. But don't let me get ahead of my story. When I started out for her house, it was drizzling. I had to drive all the way across town. She lives in Westown. And, Gilbert, how can a community like this allow itself to contain such a district? It's awful. And that talented girl living there—those rickety houses, dark, muddy streets, not even paved. Well, she *is* talented, but she's not as considerate as she might be. By the time I got to Westown, it was pouring and the wind was blowing, and I floundered around in the dark and the mud before I could find the place. I knocked on the door— this broken-down house, Gilbert, you can't imagine—and no one came. There was no porch—just broken steps up to a door—and I was getting soaked. I was sort of frightened, too, because it was so dark, and I could almost *feel* sinister figures lurking in the darkness, but I could see a dim light under the door and I kept pounding, and finally it opened. It was Miss Burkman, bundled up in a wrapper and with a piece of flannel tied around her neck. She said she was sorry but she had a bad sore throat—she did, too—so she wouldn't be able to help me out. I could have wept! Why didn't she let me know? It was the least— Still, it isn't my inconvenience that's important. I told her I was sorry and asked if I could do anything for her, and she said no, she'd be all right, and then I called her by the wrong name and got back into the car. Drenched."

Gilbert Miles said with gentle meditativeness, "Now, I wonder why you did that."

Marian picked up her stockings and felt them. They were dry, and she rolled them into a ball and put it on the chair behind her. "I didn't stop to wonder," she said. "I had a program to worry about and twenty or thirty parents, including, as you may remember, several Negroes. I drove back across town and to the school, and when I got there, the business meeting was about to begin. I sat next to a Mrs. Weintraub. John has talked about their boy, Samuel—you may remember. They're in the sixth grade together. He's that child prodigy, a mathematical genius or something, with the *very* thick lenses. Anyway, I told Mrs. Weintraub about my problem, how I had no program at all. I should have known! She's a pushy, aggressive woman, really a bundle of irrepressible, egotistic energy, and she said immediately that *she* could sing, and she could sing *Negro* songs, and she'd just run right home and get her music. I asked, 'What songs?' and—" Here Marian broke off and covered her face with her hands. When she looked up, she said, "Gilbert, honestly! The woman said, 'Oh, any of the old favorites, you know.'"

Gilbert Miles looked solemnly questioning. "Well?"

"Well! Can't you imagine? The old Uncle Tom favorites, of course! And there were two Negro mothers in the audience, and a Negro father."

"You mean—"

"I mean I had to try to stop it, of course. So I told her I couldn't think of letting her go to the trouble. She said that she lived very near the school and would *love* to! And before I could dissuade her, she was on her feet and out. I sat through the business meeting in a trance. It was awful. And in a little while she was back with sheets of music."

"Your hat's steaming," Gilbert said.

Marian snatched the hat from the fender and tossed it on the chair with the stockings. "Then I had a ray of hope. Mrs. Weintraub said she'd need someone to accompany her. I prayed—Gilbert, I honestly prayed—that there was no one besides me in that audience who could play the piano. She asked me whether I could accompany her, and I whispered back that I couldn't tell one note from another. It was my only chance. Well, the business part was over—I don't know what went on!—and Mrs. Lewis introduced me, as Program Committee. I got up, trembling, and explained our general plan, and then told how I'd been disappointed by Miss Burkman—I emphasized the fact that Miss Burkman was to sing spirituals—but that Mrs. Weintraub had proposed that she sing in her place. Then, instead of giving my little prepared talk on spirituals, I asked whether anyone would offer to accompany Mrs. Wein-traub. There was a blessed minute or two while no one volunteered, and I did no urging, believe me. But then Mrs. Weintraub herself stood up and waved her sheets of music. 'They're just the simple old favorites,' she said. 'Won't anyone play them? A child could!' And, Lord, someone volunteered! The irony! It was one of the colored women—a Mrs. Miller. She couldn't have known what she was getting into. I could have died for her. The indignity to her!"

"Oh, come, Marian, it doesn't sound bad."

"It was awful. We had 'Old Black Joe,' 'Carry Me Back to Old Virginny,' 'Dixie,' 'My Old Kentucky Home,' and 'Swanee River!' "

Gilbert laughed. "Well, now really—"

"Yes, really! I had something serious planned. I wished to show the dignity of the colored people, their artistic integrity, and a native art form! I wanted to educate those people, to make them feel— And then that stuff, instead! I *can't* forgive that Mrs. Weintraub. I don't mind the stupidity, but the sheer want of human sensitiveness!"

"Could she sing?"

"That's *not* the point! It's a matter of imagination."

"Did you thank her, dear?"

Marian nodded her head impatiently. "Of course. I had to. But, Gilbert, then I made another silly mistake. I called *her* Miss Burkman!"

Delighted incredulity broke over his face. Then he threw back his head and broke into laughter. "You *didn't*, Marian! You *couldn't!*" he shouted, bending double with enjoyment.

"I was really disappointed—and rattled."

He slapped both thighs with his hands and threw himself back in his chair. He began to choke with his merriment.

She looked at him very coolly. "After all, we can't all be detached and sharp and levelheaded, like you, darling!"

He stopped laughing. "Oh, come, now, don't be angry!"

"I'm not." She smiled wanly.

"Good. Because it *is* funny."

"I don't think it is. I think it's serious." She studied her hands in her lap, as if for an answer. Then she asked her question aloud, "Darling, what's *wrong* with the middle class?"

He looked down at her solemnly. "Which class is that, dear?"

For a moment, she did not raise her dejected head. The rain blew at the windows in an enigmatic sputter of reply, a log crackled as it fell, and, briefly, tongues of fire darted up, as if to speak, and then Marian lifted her face. Her good humor was gone, and her animation, and her comfortable, meaningless self-depreciation. He saw that she was about to cry. He jumped to his feet and stood beside her. The game was over. He pressed her head against his thigh and affectionately rumpled her damp hair. "Pussycat!" he said comfortingly.

DOG

I suppose that we were shaken, my brother and I, told to wake up, come down. I have a clear recollection of clinging to the banister, coming down that steep, freezing flight of stairs in our flannel nightgowns in winter.

And I remember our being down there, in the kitchen, with the wood-burning range by then roaring away and the room very warm, and my brother and I hoisted up on some low stand or a table, and both of us having our faces and hands roughly washed and each of us being dressed, one by our grandmother, the other by our mother, in the tolerable kitchen heat.

But where were the men? Presumably off already, attending to their affairs. My grandfather had some kind of cattle brokerage business, and at that time would still harness up his horse early in the day and drive off into the country in his buggy, or, in winter, his sleigh with its cheerful harness bells. My father was the manager of a new canning company. My grandmother had her little notions shop on the main street, and after she departed presently for her business, my mother was left to take care of the household.

This may in fact be the reason that my father moved into that house when he married her. My mother had (she often told me in later years) been the drudge, while her enterprising elders saw to their enterprises; and then her husband, another enterpriser, and she, with two small boys, still took care of the house as for some years she had.

My notion of a money shortage must be mistaken. I know that my father (for all the bareness in which his mother and older brother lived in their little cottage down near the canning factory) was one of the first people in that town to own an automobile. I can almost believe that I remember the first, a Rush, purple. I do remember the second, a Ford—bright red, a two-seater, very high, very short, with shiny brass fittings and a round gasoline tank perched up behind the seat. I well remember the third, a dark-blue Reo touring car; but that was after we had moved into our own house. The local photographer was called one Sunday to take our touring picture (it exists): the top down, both veiled grandmothers in the back seat, a SAUK CITY pennant strung along it; my father in a beige duster at the wheel, wearing a cap; my mother, also veiled, beside him; my brother popping his head up in the back; I hiding on the floor to find out, idiotically, whether the camera, still an object of mystery to me, would, like an X-ray eye, show me there.

But before we left our grandparents' house there must have been a number of automobiles in that town. We had a dachshund named Tighe, the only pet that I remember in those years, who was run over and killed by a car in front of that house. The car could hardly have been moving at more than twenty miles an hour, but Tighe was killed. I remember my father picking up the limp dog but nothing about the careless driver; remember, though, my brother and me howling in grief, standing there at the roadside.

THE FACE

WITHIN

THE FACE

"Don't" Laura Newman said, too sharply for the occasion, and Robert, her husband, who had just begun to trace a light imaginary line along her smooth brown thigh, pulled his hand away and fell back on the sand. Laura did not move. In a white swimming suit, she lay stretched out on a white towel, as arranged and quiet as a statue, hair flowing back, eyes closed, lips a little parted, face and body gleaming, offering herself to the sun as supine marble figures on monuments coldly offer themselves to God.

On the sand beyond his father, staring out at the sea, sat David, their thirteen-year-old son, who looked over toward his mother speculatively now and asked, "Don't what?"

"She was talking to me," Robert said. He stretched out and, leaning on his elbow, looked gloomily down at his wife's ear—an object strange and perfect, as if wrought, like an artifact, by cautious, astonishing skill. He turned away, toward the boy. "Let's swim," he said.

Laura did not speak or move. *Burn, burn,* she was thinking, *burn, burn, burn,* in the rhythm of the small, lapping waves that endlessly, warmly buffeted the yellow shore. The perfect, paradoxical, immaculate pleasure as the hot sun burns and burns on the skin! The accumulated and clinging irritations and frustrations and dismal intensities of four wet and cold winter months seemed to dry upon her and fall away like scales, and she could almost feel herself emerging, with this hot balm, new and absolutely pure, and in her mind she linked the images, from a forgotten school poem, of fire and ice.

She could hear, high above her or far out over the blue cove, the distant, whimpering cry of gulls—shrill whispers—and behind her closed lids she pictured them wheeling in silvery arcs against the cool blue of the sky. Nearer, traveling along the sand to her ear, she heard the swishing sound of feet as Robert and David went down to the water. Then she heard them splashing. Then she thought, *Puberty,* and at once, with the thought, she shuddered, and her warm skin was chilled, as if the sun had gone under a cloud and a cold wind abruptly blew.

"You should take him South with you if you can manage," Mr. Lowell, the headmaster, had written. "He is well along toward puberty now, you know, growing a little too fast, and he needs some sun, needs to be built up. He's not a rugged boy by nature. Of course, we would be glad to keep him here at the school during the spring holiday—he's a most likable and tractable lad, and I'm confident that the arrangements could be made—but in his own interest we all feel that you should consider taking him with you." And so on, and, of course, there had been no question but that the headmaster was right, only there had been the somewhat irritating question of revising their plans, of cutting their three weeks to a little less than two. Yet here they were, their sixth gorgeous day, and she expressed her grati-

tude to the sun in a luxurious arching of her back and
stretching of her toes, until her body was taut with pleasure. Into this momentary intense delight, voices broke.
She relaxed and slowly turned, and raised her head and
shoulders with her elbows under her.

Robert and David were still in the water, Rober swimming briskly out, David standing still, water to his knees, a
bony little figure in the forefront of the vast expanse of
empty sea. Turning her head, she saw that other people
had come and were settling themselves on the sand at a
barely reasonable distance behind her—a man and woman
and two girls and a boy.

Laura swore softly. On their first day, the Newmans
had wandered away from the big stretch of beach in front of
their hotel and had found this quiet cove, where the surf
broke far out and where almost no one ever came. They
had enjoyed the empty sea from the small, empty beach
fringed with barren dunes, where there was no intrusion of
strident voices, no gross intimacy with other bodies. Then
who were these people disposing themselves now on the
sand just behind her, already shouting and calling and
shrilling, the mother to her scattering children, the husband to the wife? Not, Laura thought, guests of the hotel.

She stared at them. The man wore droopy, flowered
trunks. He had a long, skinny white body, with a scrawny
patch of black hair on his white chest, and black forearms
and legs, and a narrow head with too much black hair
above his ears, and the white scalp showing through the
thin hair on top. The wife was short and round, with a
round head and, again, too much black, untidy hair. The
children were like their mother—short and round, with
round heads and faces, the girls with fuzzy black pigtails,
the boy with a black shock that stood up in ragged thrusts.
The man was pulling towels from a basket and spreading
them on the sand, and when the wife had seated herself on

one, she reached into the basket and brought out a tube, and Laura watched her spread a thick layer of white salve over her nose, under her eyes, and on her cheekbones, so that she suddenly gave the fantastic impression of wearing a white domino that had been cut in half. Then Laura saw that something was wrong with her right arm; it seemed, somehow, crippled, the fingers that applied the ointment knotted in a queer way and the elbow not quite free. And when, suddenly, she shouted to her children, who had run down to the water, her face, too, or the right side of it, showed some similar defect—a partial paralysis, which made her seem to leer. When she stopped shouting, her face settled into what was apparently its perpetual expression—a horrid, rigid simper.

Laura shuddered with distaste, turned around and sat up, and determinedly faced the sea. Two things she passionately claimed as belonging to her life, and she wanted them in small no less than large ways. They were privacy and self-possession. At this moment, in a small way, this family had snatched the second with the first. As she watched Robert helping David with his crawl in the quiet water of the cove, she wondered irritably how people such as these could disturb her composure, until, in a sudden misery of recollection, she knew that it was because of their disgusting domesticity; somehow they gave the impression of having brought their entire household onto the immaculate beach, spilled out on the sand the whole steamy clutter of their lives, so that Laura thought of a cantankerous parrot in a parlor cage, some potted ferns before stiff lace curtains, a kitchen sink full of greasy dishes, and soiled bed linen, gray.

Laura sat stiffly on the sand in the abrupt and heavy grip of a life long since dead—of a sordid beach town in New Jersey, of a cheap, flimsily built cottage, a girl lying at night with her head under her pillow to shut out the sounds that came through the walls from the bedroom next to hers, and the girl in the day, seeking out some lonely place on the beach where she could lie in the sun for hours, unmolested, to purge herself. The people behind her, by their presence alone, had destroyed her careful peace, and through closed teeth she swore in anger, because now the sun was helpless.

The woman was screaming at the boy, who had walked down to the water and was watching Robert and David. "Lou-ee! Lou-ee!" she shrilled, and then some word that came to Laura as "Ny-ah! Ny-ah!"—like an abstraction from all negatives. Laura glanced over her shoulder at the distorted mouth under the white mask, and the stiff arm gesticulating, and then, turning back, lowered her head into her cupped hands, so that she sat with her fingers pressed over her ears. Yet she could hear the father, calling more gently, "Lou-ee, come!" The boy stared at his parents and, at last, laggingly, came back to where they sat. Laura heard his grunt as he flung himself on the sand behind her, saying, "What's the fun? What'd we come for?" The mother said, "Just wait," and the father said, "We'll go in soon."

Dripping, gleaming in the sun, Robert and David came out of the water, up the sand. "We have company," Laura said quietly when they stood before her. With identical indifference in their eyes, they looked at the group behind her. "What's wrong with the woman's face and arm, Robert?" she asked with whispered irritation.

"I don't know," Robert said. He dropped to the sand and sat cross-legged beside her towel, at her feet. David duplicated the position at her other side.

"Ny-ah, ny-ah!" the woman called out to one of her little girls, who was digging in the sand and scattering it. Involuntarily, Laura glanced at her again.

"Some slight paralysis," Robert said, his face turned away, and Laura, watching the stiff arm stuck out with its twisted fingers, said "Ugh!" and turned away, too.

Briskly Robert said, "Well, David's getting good," but even when he leaned over and slapped the boy lightly on the shoulder in congratulation, David continued to stare at the woman and then let his eyes move to the white-faced boy who sat near her, sifting sand through his fingers.

"Aren't you, David?" Robert said loudly.

"What?" the boy asked vaguely, blinking suddenly as he looked at his father.

"Your crawl. It's good."

"Oh."

The blank indifference in David's voice made Laura shift her gaze from the glinting sea to the boy's impassive face. Once more he was staring at the people behind her while his hands, too, idly sifted sand. Then, as she looked at him, she saw that some subtle difference had overtaken his features since she had last really studied them. He was on the way to becoming a different boy. Since his last holiday, she thought, his neck had visibly lengthened, and all the bones of his face had coarsened—the jaw longer, the cheekbones more prominent, the forehead higher. And yet he was still a little boy. It was almost as if, within the hairless, child's face, another face was pushing through. That was a man's face. It was—she glanced at her husband—it was, indeed, Robert's face. *Puberty*, she thought, staring at the boy with a kind of horror. She saw him lengthening out and broadening, the chest swelling, the arms swelling, nails thickening, hair—and her legs and arms were suddenly covered with goose flesh, shivering prickles sweeping her skin as, for the first time, she recognized in him the gross, inevitable thrust into manhood.

Then, behind her, the woman began noisily to scold, and Laura, who was clutching her arms to her sides, as if she were cold, lay back and tried to relax, closed her eyes once more, and sought to regain her private exchange with the sun, her perfect isolation in light. But she was too aware of everything around her to capture that pure sensation of complete and separate being. Even as her body warmed and her skin began to burn, she heard the people behind her moving about, preparing at last to go down to the water, and the sounds of running and sliding in the sand and their shifting cries told her when they went. Robert and David were talking together in low voices, and then she was aware of David's moving off a bit and beginning to dig in the sand. She heard the distant sound of splashing water, of voices laughing and shouting, of David's hands digging, slapping wet sand, scraping, and she felt Robert's eyes on her as he still sat at her feet.

Then he spoke. "What do you think of David?" he asked.

She lay completely quiet. "Think of him?"

"We haven't talked about him. How do you think he is?"

"I think he's fine. Don't you?"

"No. I think we should bring him home."

She sat up abruptly. "What did you say, Robert?" The sun seemed to blind her as she tried to see his face.

"The end of this term would be a good time to break. Bring him back to a school in the city."

"But why *break* from a good school to a less good one? There's no city school that—"

"The schooling part isn't all that matters. He needs us. He needs a home."

"David? He's thirteen! He's been away for three years. What does he need with us now? I've just thought— he's—why, he's nearly a man . . ."

"He's lonely."

"Lonely? David?"

"Lonely. Yes. It hurts me."

She looked at him with blind eyes, staring, and he said, "A man? He's nearly a *man?*"

With this question, the mad shimmering of the sun suddenly died, and she saw him clearly. He was *there*, thin and clear and brown and tractable. She said, "Yes. After all, only four or five more years . . . Just now, I could see *you* in him, emerging. He's a big boy. He *needs* to be away from home. He shouldn't have to depend on us now. What can we do for him?"

"Everything we've never done," Robert said.

"I don't know what you're talking about."

"He doesn't seem to have any anchorage. Least of all in us. He's adrift—lost in himself some way."

She said curtly, "Nonsense."

He looked at her steadily before he spoke. "You're so beautiful," he said at last, almost as if he were meditating upon a theory, and then he went on quietly, "But something's wrong with our life. I don't know what it is, but . . ."

"But?" she asked.

"But . . ."

"Yes?"

He began to run his hands through the sand aimlessly, letting the grains sift slowly between his fingers. She watched him, and at last she said, "Well, that's gratitude!" She looked away from him to the running figures on the shore—the man and his wife and the three children, in and out of the water at the shallow edge of beach, shouting and ridiculously running. "I thought that we lived the way you wanted. I thought we had a—"

"We have," he said for her. "It's a beautiful, smooth, perfectly organized life. But what's missing?"

"Is anything?"

"Well, for example, whatever it is that David ought to feel about you."

"I don't know what you're talking about."

"Do you think you know him?"

"Of course."

"Look," Robert said. "Does he ever *talk* to you? Do you know what he's thinking about? Do you know what he's *like?*"

Laura looked at him. "It's you—I don't know what *you're* like," she said.

"Ahh!" he said, a long, disparaging denial, and turned away from her.

She lay back and began to cry. With a certain luxury, she felt the tears push up through her locked lids and run down and over her cheeks. They must be dropping on her towel! She said, "At last. I knew it would come sometime—it had to—and now it has. You—always so reservedly kind and unclaiming. Now, at last, you're using your position that until now you've hardly ever admitted. Now you tell me that I've failed—from *my* position!"

"Position?" he cried. "Oh, my God!"

She felt her tears burning on her skin, and, eyes still closed, she said, "Don't exclaim. I know it's true. I've always waited. I knew it would come someday. *My* inadequacy. So now it's come." Then, roughly brushing her cheeks with her fingers, she sat up. She tossed her hair back and cried, "But why today? Why, on the day that . . ." She looked to the water's edge, where the other family, gathered in a group, was starting back up the beach. "Why today, with those people here?"

He glanced at them. "What of them? What have they got to do with anything?" And, looking back at her, he cried, "Oh, look, don't be a fool!" Then he came through the sand on his knees and seized her hands. He held them and rubbed them and looked at her blurred brown eyes. "Laura, don't be a fool," he said, and, hearing the protestation of love in these unlikely words, she looked away from him and down at the sand. She detached her hands. She felt the sun burn on her shoulders. She lifted her face a little and felt the sun blessedly burn away the dampness around her eyelids. She looked out to the sea—the miles of blue, endless blue, nothing but blue, and over it the interminable reaches of cool blue sky—and she looked back at Robert, anxious beside her, and said with slow ease, "I'm sorry."

"I am, too."

"But you agree, don't you, that David shouldn't be taken from his school?"

Robert looked past her face and said, "David's heard. Perhaps all of it," and when Laura turned, she saw that, yes, there he was, only twelve or fifteen feet away from them, his hands deep in the bowels of a sand castle, stopped there for Lord knew how long, and his face turned toward them, his eyes wide and watchful. She could think of nothing to say except "They're coming back."

The others were just passing David. They had walked in a group from the shore, the mother in the lead, her foolish round face, encumbered with its unintended grin and its ridiculous swath of white ointment, lifted as she led her throng, her tribe. Behind her was the skinny, hairy, fish-white husband, behind him the homely little girls and, lagging now at David's castle, the boy. He stopped there and watched while the others went on, until David made some gesture of invitation, and then he dropped to his knees and both began silently to dig. The rest of the family settled itself again in its place, and when the little girls began a tentative movement toward the boys, the mother said sharply, "Ny-ah! Esther! Mir!" Reluctantly, they turned back and sat on the sand beside her.

Laura looked away from her. "What mad possessiveness," she said.

The two boys were standing over the castle now, facing the sea, and the strange boy asked David a question, which he answered by ducking his head, hunching his shoulders, and moving his arms in the motion of the crawl. The other boy imitated him. Then, talking, they moved down to the water, and both ran in. David swam and the other boy watched, but only for a moment. Then the boy's mother was on her feet and screaming again, "Ny-ah! Ny-ah! Lou-ee! Come!" Her right cheek was distorted in her excitement, and her injured arm flailed grotesquely at the air.

The boy turned slowly and looked at her. Now, at last, he was outraged. Over the bright distance, Laura could see the fury in his tense white face. He did not look back at David but came walking with slow deliberation up the beach, past the Newmans, whose heads turned as he walked, to his mother, who was still shaking her hand at him. Then, standing perhaps six feet before her, his arms flailing, too, but in a rage, he yelled at her, "Ny-ah! Ny-ah! Ny-ah!"

She looked at him in amazement for a moment and then seemed to wilt. All the perky animation left her round body as she turned slowly and settled saggingly on her towel and, at last, sinking prone, with her face pressed into its folds, wept. Her husband hurried to her, and Laura looked back to the sea. She saw David standing in the shallow water, watching intently, and then, glancing at his lifted hand, move his fingers experimentally. Then he started back to them.

The husband, kneeling beside his wife with his arm over her shoulders, murmured consolingly to her, and her sobs began to subside. The boy, quiet now, with a kind of shamed determination on his face, stood stiffly on the spot where he had faced her. Then the father summoned him with an uncompromising gesture, until the boy moved reluctantly to her. There were words that the Newmans could not hear, but the boy presently knelt beside his mother, where his father had been, and spoke softly to her. Then the mother swiftly twisted to a sitting position, her contorted face red, and seizing the boy in her arms, she broke again into sobs as she embraced him in a convulsion of love.

"My God! Let's go," Laura said, and leaped up. Hastily Robert helped her put their belongings in their beach basket, and without looking at the other family again, they walked away as rapidly as the loose sand allowed. Only David, lagging behind his parents, kept looking back, until the dunes cut off his view.

On the way to the hotel, the Newmans did not talk much, and they did not mention the other family, but a few hours later, when Laura was brushing her hair before a tall triple mirror in the dressing-room alcove off her bedroom, she suddenly exclaimed, "I can't get them out of my mind!"

Robert was sitting on the edge of her bed, leafing through a magazine, and he looked up and asked, "Who?"

"That awful family—that woman."

"Oh."

David, who was lying on his back on a chaise longue, his legs flung out in masculine abandon, was doing something with his hands, which he held close before his face. Apparently preoccupied with his fingers and oblivious of his parents, he nevertheless now said quietly, "They weren't bad."

"That man's—*drawers!* That's all you can call them."

Robert laughed, but David asked in an innocent tone, "Just ordinary trunks, weren't they?" He rolled over on his stomach, as if to study his hands more closely.

Laura said, "You could hardly blame the boy for screaming back at her."

David said, "The boy was O.K. I like him."

Laura watched him in the glass. "What are you doing, David?"

He stood up lazily. "Nothing," he said. He walked to a window and leaned against the frame, and then he was fooling with his fingers again.

Suddenly Laura saw what he was doing. "Stop it, David!" she said sharply.

Robert looked up again. "What's the matter?"

She watched David closely. He was standing by the window in such a way that the late-afternoon sunlight made a nimbus of the down on one cheek and along his chin. She thought of that down as a precursor to coarse stubble, and she said, "David, get out of here, will you? You make me nervous. Go wash your face."

"It's clean," he said as he started toward the door. He watched her with empty eyes as he sidled away.

Robert moved, and presently he was standing behind her. She looked up in the central mirror and met his sad, inquiring, forgiving eyes. "What was he doing?" Robert asked.

"I think he was trying to make his fingers look para-lyzed, like that grotesque woman's."

Robert laughed uneasily. "Curiosity, probably. You know boys—they're interested in oddity. Probably not at all grotesque to him. Perhaps the contrary. Rather fasci-nating."

Laura brushed her hair with renewed vigor, until she had counted ten, twenty, thirty strokes. "He practically said he liked them."

"Well," Robert allowed, "perhaps he did."

Her brush paused in her hair. "Is it time for a drink?"

"I'll get you one." But he did not go. He put his hands on her shoulders and stroked her upper arms. "You are beautiful," he said.

For a moment or two, she sat immobile, unprotesting, under his hands. Then she said, "What about that drink?" She watched his reflection move away, and when he was out of the room, she leaned toward the mirror, toward her reflection. Her face cleared, as if shadows were passing from it, as if shadows had vanished from the shadows of her mind, and she smiled.

She opened a drawer of the dressing table and took out two gold bracelets—one with square chunks of jewels held in heavy links, and one with coins the size of half dollars—and put one on each wrist. Late sunlight shone upon her and flashed off the chains and the jewels in darting angles on the glass surfaces around her. Then, in the triple mirror, she caught sight of a figure moving. It was David again—moving, stopping. She watched his reflection. He was looking not at her but at his right hand, as he held it before him and forced his fingers into an imitation of gnarled paralysis.

"David," she said quietly, "please don't do that. Why do you keep doing that?"

He looked up and met her eyes in the mirror. "I just want to know how it feels," he said. "That woman—how she feels."

"If her hand is paralyzed, she probably doesn't feel anything. And why should you want to know how *she* feels?"

"I kind of liked her." He looked at Laura blandly.

"She was so loud—screaming all the time."

"They just weren't used to a beach, that was all. She was worried."

Laura lifted her hands to fasten a gold barrette in her brushed hair so that one ear would show, but she still watched David manipulating his fingers.

Suddenly his face brightened. At last, he had duplicated the crippled arm. "This is the way it feels!"

Her eyes searched the mirror until his glance met hers. Then she grimaced in disgust and said with sharp finality, "Don't be perverse! She was—ugly!"

David was standing rigid behind her. His arm rose until it pointed out at her with a stiff, accusing crook at the elbow and in the clumsy-knuckled fingers. His drawn face was stiff with revulsion, only his eyes alive, glimmering upon her. "Says who?" he asked in a dead voice, and as his wild, unhappy eyes held and held hers, her bracelets clanked down on the mirrored top of the dressing table with a metallic chorus, and the mirrors flashed.

SCHOOL

I can date quite closely the time of our leaving my grandparents' house for our own. When my brother was in the first grade at school—the school was about a block and a half away—I wanted to go, too, and would scream and yell to no avail. One day in 1912 I decided that I *would* go and I ran after him when he left, but while he managed to clear the picket fence that surrounded that property, I did not, and was caught on it by my pants while he chased away up the street. Someone came out and picked me off and put me down. But my mother must have talked to the teacher, because then, for the rest of that year—it was probably late in the spring—I *was* allowed to go to school. I sat in front of the rows of benches (the first three grades were in one room) and was allowed to try to work along with the first grade, at whatever they were doing. The teacher was named Nellie Welch, a very fine lady. That is the last recollection that I have of still living in that house, although certainly I spent a good deal of time in it over the following years.

My father's father died when Father was three years old, in La Crosse. That means that his younger brother,

George, was one, and his older brother, Joseph, five. The three boys and their widowed mother came to Sauk City in, one supposes, 1904. How she had held that family together through those years, I have no idea. There are so many things one should have asked about but didn't even really think about. At any rate, my father was born in 1878, so he was twenty-six years old when they arrived. (My mother was five years older.) Whether they came there because Father had been offered a job in the canning factory, I again don't know, but their little house was very near the factory, and by the time he married, he was the manager of the company. His brother George almost at once had established himself in a similar position in another canning factory at Baraboo, and had moved up there. Joe, a man of retarded intellect if not in fact a moron, stayed in Sauk City and was for most of his life a kind of straw boss in the factory.

When I legally entered the first grade in 1913, we had already moved into the house, about a block away from theirs, that my grandparents had built for us. It cost $5,000, a sum often mentioned in awe as vast, and so it was at that time in that town, and the house did seem to be full of splendor, especially by way of what seemed to be extraordinarily lavish chandeliers, art nouveau, in the dining room and living room, and in a statue fixture at the turn of the broad front stairway—we always used the narrower back flight—up to the second floor.

The statue was dark bronze, a Grecian-like figure holding up a bunch of grapes in one hand, a tray of them on her other arm, and three small frosted bulbs riding on brackets from behind her head. It fascinated me as a child, and many years later, it fascinated my then small son Page in the same way. When I went back to Wisconsin in 1967 for my father's funeral, and we were to clear out that house for sale, my son begged me to rescue that fixture for him. It was the only thing I took from that sad house. Page has it now in his house in Berkeley, très chic, but it gives me no pleasure.

PICKING UP
THE PIECES

It was early summer, and the windows and doors were open, and when Harry Calder raised his voice and shouted, "All right, then, yes, goddamn it, I did!" the little girl next door abruptly stopped her piano practice. And Liza Calder, having forced her husband to this extraordinary admission, did not know what to do; she did not even know what to feel. She stood helpless in the middle of the sudden silence, and as her fingers slowly went limp with the rest of her body, the letter she had been holding fluttered to the floor. She looked around the room, and for a moment she could not decide why it seemed so strange. Then she saw that it was as if Harry's shout had blown this familiar and carefully planned room apart. Every object in it stood out separately from every other object, in a kind of crazy isolation—the chintz-covered chairs, the little lacquered tables, Harry himself, the ashtrays and books, even the prints of birds and flowers that hung in rows on the walls—everything was separated from everything else, without relationship. A trick of her eyes, she thought, and blinked hard, but her second thought was, No; rather, the pieces of her marriage.

She looked down at the floor, where the letter lay, pale blue and innocent against the dark, polished wood, almost as if she expected to see scattered fragments, as if Harry's shout had been, in fact, a dropped plate. And then she began at last to cry softly, and sank down into one of the unattached chairs.

Exactly at that moment, the little girl next door, apparently deciding that there were to be no more interesting sounds from the Calders' living room, began to play again. "Tink, tink-le, tink-le, tink, tink, tink" went the piano, tentatively, in a jerky, uncertain movement. For the twentieth time that day, she was beginning the easiest of Bach's minuets for children. And Liza, even now, found herself listening, even helping the child along in her mind. *Tink*, her mind said, *tink*, tink-le, tink-le, *tink*, tink, tink—giving the phrase its accents. And then, as though they communicated across the grass, the flower beds, the hedge, the little girl got it, too, and the piano sounded out the simple phrase with nice authority, and maintained it in the next. Liza blew her nose and wiped her eyes.

Harry spoke first. "Well, now what?"

She glanced at him where he sat on the edge of the sofa, like someone in a doctor's waiting room. He did not look ashamed; he merely looked angry, as though she had unfairly put him in a frustrating position. She began to cry again, and said, "That's that, that's all."

"What do you mean by that?"

"I mean—" and she jumped to her feet and swept up the letter from the floor. She read aloud the cloying sentence that had revealed his guilt, and while she began it with an acid simper in her voice, she ended it with distraught flatness. " 'Now in the summer again,' " she read, " 'the Common and the Public Gardens are lovely, with the full green trees and the yellow evening light under them, and I can't resist writing just to tell you that I often wish, as I cross through after work, that you would be the one waiting in the Ritz bar.' Well," Liza concluded angrily, "I mean that you're free now to go up to Boston and sit in the Ritz bar and wait for her or anyone else you feel like waiting for. I'm through."

"You're crazy," he said faintly.

The thin music began again—the opening phrases precise, the next two stumbling; then the music stopped again. Involuntarily Liza looked out through the open French doors toward the house next door, whose white gables jutted up among elm trees. She saw a hummingbird darting in and out of the brilliant-blue larkspur that grew proudly along the privet, and even from her distance she could see the blue reflected as brilliantly on the gleaming feathers of the bird's tiny breast. The sight made her burst into new sobs, but sadly now, no longer in rage. And the music began once more, with its *tink-le, tink-le, tink-le.*

"How could I go on?" she cried. "What's left to go on *on?"*

Harry stood up, and now he seemed altogether too large for the room. "Nothing is any different," he said impatiently.

"Trust—" she said weakly.

"Look," he said. "If you hadn't found that letter— let's say if you hadn't *read* that letter—"

"I wouldn't have known! But now I *do* know."

"It happened twelve months ago. You've been living with me for a year since then, and nothing seemed different to you from the seven years before that one. Nothing *was* different."

The little girl's piano was different, Liza could hear. The little girl had just gone through the first sixteen bars of her minuet without once stumbling, and now she was repeating them with even greater confidence. "*Tum,* tum-tum-tum-tum, *tum,* tum, tum" came the familiar notes, but dropping now with a new kind of emphasis and depth, with a certain weight, through the summer air. Then, when the child came to the first of the second sixteen bars, her fingers failed her again. She stopped, and when she began again, a moment later, she had reduced her tempo and went slowly, almost painfully, into the second part. The treble notes were higher, and once more the music sounded thin and almost as aimless as birds' chirrups.

"How could anything have been really the same?" Liza asked as she saw that she still held the pale-blue letter and that she had been staring at the spidery handwriting without seeing it. She put it carefully down on the table beside her chair, put it down not as though it were something that might break but, rather, as though it were something that might bite her—some corrupt little animal, perhaps. Then Harry came stomping across the room so heavily that the glass pendants on the wall brackets above the mantel trembled. He took the letter, tore it up into small pieces, and dropped the pieces into the fireplace, where they lay like forget-me-nots on the dark-green laurel leaves that filled the hearth.

"That's just how important that thing was," he said, and he kicked at the branches, so that the light pieces of paper fell off the leaves and disappeared among them.

"They're still there. They're just covered up," Liza said quietly.

"I've almost never thought of that girl since I was up there."

"Tell me something, Harry," Liza said then, with quite reasonableness. "What did you think of me?"

"You mean—then?"

"Yes."

"I didn't. That's just the point. It didn't have anything to do with you, with us, with our marriage."

"It had to do with you."

"I was up there for three weeks. You were here. I saw this girl every day, because I was reorganizing the office in which she worked. She was pleasant—friendly. We had drinks together a couple of times. It was just about like that."

"As though you weren't married, in short?"

He glanced at her suspiciously. 'Well, yes, in a way."

"But you were."

Now he took up her tone of patient reasonableness. "What is a marriage like ours, anyway? Something that can be messed up by—nothing? By a—well, a mere *episode?* I hope not. I—why, listen, Liza, it's the whole pattern of my life. You know that."

"Pattern," Liza said thoughtlessly, merely echoing him, and she looked out of the windows again. Now there were two hummingbirds in the larkspur, and the child next door was slowly putting together the phrases of the second sixteen bars. She stumbled on a little run but, without stopping, went neatly into a series of six staccato quarter notes, to a firmly held whole note, and then, with an adequate glissando in the left hand, into the eight final measures, played *piano.*

Liza turned her eyes back to Harry. He stood before her, large and square-shouldered, with his hands thrust aggressively into his pockets, but his face looked helpless, hindered. She stood up, so that he would not seem so big. Behind him, the convex glass in the gilt-framed, eagle-mounted cabochon mirror sparkled with sunlight, and in it Liza could see nearly the entire room and, much reduced in size, the back of Harry's head and shoulders and her own flushed face, then, in microscopic perfection, even the small objects of the room—a crystal vase giving back the gleam; a silver cigarette lighter, in a Regency pattern, like a large jewel; a green jade elephant reflected in black lacquer —and then the French doors behind her, and the blue flowers against the hedge outside, and the white gables of the house next door, among the leafy branches. She took her eyes off the mirror, and she saw that at some point the room had pulled itself together again. It was a harmonious room, restful, and decorated with meticulous taste, and, really, it was true, nothing jarred now—nothing at all. And when Harry suddenly spoke again, saying gently, "Look, can you imagine *not* being married to me?" she knew that she could not, and she said, as she burst into tears once more and plopped down into the chair again, "No, damn it, I can't."

He was on his knees beside her in an instant, and he put his arms around her clumsily and pressed her head against his shoulder. "Darling, don't!" he tenderly urged. "That thing's dead. It won't happen again. Please don't cry any more. Listen, Liza . . ."

She cried comfortably on his shoulder, and then, as she abruptly raised her head to hear, she murmured, with relief, "Listen, she's got it!"

And, indeed, the little girl had. She played through the minuet from beginning to end—"*tum*, tum-tum-tum-tum, *tum*, tum, tum"—in a nearly flawless, if still rather mechanical, performance, with precise accentuation, phrasing, timing. Both Liza and Harry smiled for her. You could shut your eyes and almost imagine that the little girl was really good.

T E N S I O N

*O*nce we were in our own house, the "parlor" tradition was maintained, but with some alleviation. Closed most of the time, that stiffly furnished "parlor"—I can remember only a mahogany settee and two matching rocking chairs, a mahogany bookcase containing a few dozen strange books (dead kaisers laid out in state, tropical beasts, etc.), and an upright piano. It was the piano that unlocked the double doors and let some warmth into that room. My mother played the piano, not well but adequately, and sang rather prettily in a high soprano. She had had ambitions, as a girl, to become a professional singer. My father liked to sing, too, in his strained tenor way. And when they were content —on Sunday evenings, I think—they would open the parlor and play and sing, and my brother and I would be with them in that little-used room, listening to them, and looking through some of those strange, seldom examined, always mysterious books.

Those were pleasant interludes in a childhood not always pleasant.

I wish that I could define the horrid tension that at most times positively vibrated in our house, that thing between my mother and my father that can't have been as simple as I have always thought it to be: his sense of having been betrayed into marriage. Whatever it was, he would behave very badly, enigmatically (to my brother and me) taunting her until he had driven her into a desperate frenzy, so that even on ghastly winter nights she would at last leap up and rush out of the house crying, "I'll jump off the bridge!" (She would have jumped on ice only about eight feet below the bridge, breaking some bones; still, the threat was dreadful; and usually, in the spring, the river was high, sometimes flooding, and she could well have been swept away.) My father would do nothing, just sit there. A half dozen times, at least, I went streaking out after her, in weather icy or balmy, and caught up with her a half block away, begging her to come back, half dragging her back . . .

THE LONELY
CONSTELLATION

The pretty blond girl at the grand piano in the Kitty Hawk Bar was playing old songs of the twenties and thirties in a pleasantly desultory way, and Henry Sherman heard them without quite listening. He was a roadman for a Boston publishing firm, he lived outside Chicago, he was waiting at La Guardia to connect with a plane West, and he was vaguely thinking of his return home after a three-day sales conference in Boston. Wearing a light raincoat, he sat on a stool at the round bar, his shoulders hunched over a highball, his cheek resting on his palm. He looked across the bar at the white evening light on the water outside, and at the great gray metal birds rushing across the strip of land beside it now and then and lifting themselves ponderously into the silvery twilight sky. He was tired and just slightly drunk and just slightly melancholy.

He would get into Chicago around midnight and take a late train out to Winnetka. When he got to his house, it would be late, and he would not wake his wife. She would be sleeping heavily in her bed, making a soft sound that was neither quite breathing nor yet snoring, and he would undress in his "den" and make no noise as he turned down the blue candlewick spread on his bed; yet his presence alone might stir her sleep just enough to make her turn over from her back to her side, and then the puffing sound would cease and he might be able to get in a good seven hours before the Sunday clatter of the household began.

A series of casual arpeggios carried the piano into a deft treble account of "Tea for Two," and the old song, only half recognized as it mingled with Henry's thoughts of home, somehow heightened his nearly total disinclination to return to his family. He went back there out of pure physical habit, the way a plow horse goes back to the barn, doggedly, and for a change, this self-knowledge did not shame him, it simply saddened him. Perhaps his children seemed so distant from him because he had been away from home so much, working his repetitive rounds through that vast Middle Western area, season after season for ten years now, so that he was half a stranger to them and they to him. His son was a fourteen-year-old prig who looked with disapproval on Henry's highball before dinner; "Hi-Y-and-Handsome," by way of a nickname, was Henry's occasional joke, but the boy was not amused. His daughter, Mary, looking at him owlishly through her spectacles, once in a while expressed an interest in his work by asking him questions about publishing, yet the real reason, Henry knew perfectly well, was that she was interested above everything else in the publication issued by her high school, on which she served in some devoted editorial capacity. Were they really, as they seemed to him now, children peculiarly devoid of charm and grace, or did he think so only because they gave him an increasingly strong feeling that he was an intruder in his own domain? His wife, at any rate, did not seem to notice the character of his position in the household. She went through her wifely duties with a blind, unspirited humility that made everything more drab.

Those dripping arpeggios again, and then the piano suddenly made him sit up straight on his stool. The girl was playing a song called "Tenderly." Henry had heard it two nights before in a South Boston café where it had been sung by a lithe colored girl in a long, clinging dress of green metal cloth. She had not really sung it; she had whispered it, with a fixed, unhappy smile, into a loudspeaker, her white teeth shining, her shining chocolate-brown shoulders and bosom lifting and falling in the slow rhythm of the music, over the low top of her dress. It was a queer song that kept shifting into minor tones, and it was full of all kinds of misery that was not in the words, and when the girl had come for the first time to the lines about taking my lips, taking my love, Henry Sherman had felt the back of his neck go shiveringly cold.

He listened closely now to the piano without any of that former uneasiness, trying to learn the tune, but he did not have the kind of ear that could readily retain a tune of any complexity, and this blond girl did not go on playing it over and over, as the colored girl had sung it over and over, chorus after rueful chorus, and always with that rigidly disconsolate smile, but started to play something else.

Henry looked at his watch. It was twenty minutes before his flight. He finished his drink (the third since dinner), slid off the stool, and went down to the lower level of the terminal. He went out into the arcade, paused at the desk where his flight would presently be called and where he had already checked in, and then wandered on toward the gate designated on his pass. When he came to the gate, he decided to wait a while, even though at just that moment the voice on the public-address system announced that passengers for his flight would now please board the plane.

Henry traveled a good deal by air, and he liked air travel in every way but one; over and over he had found himself stuck with some dull character in the seat beside him, and there was no way of choosing again, or of getting away, as you could on a train. Henry liked to talk with people, but he had found that some were dull and some didn't like to talk. So now he decided to wait and watch the passengers who got on this plane and follow someone who might conceivably be interesting. A few foreign-looking individuals who had been waiting at the gate when Henry came up to it had already gone out on the field, and now a man and a woman and another man, all unpromising, came along in a straggling line. But where, Henry wondered as he continued to wait, were the usual rush and concentrated push? Then one man did come running, a comic little figure with a briefcase in one hand flapping against his leg, an oversize panama held down on his head with the other hand. He ran past the gate, then came to a sliding stop, wheeled, glared frantically at the number above his head, wheeled again, and darted out on the field. Henry looked at his watch. It was five minutes before flight time, and unless some passengers had gone out through another gate, it seemed likely that quite a few were going to miss the plane. Then the voice over the public-address system gave its final call, and Henry himself passed through the gate.

Twilight was gone now, and the field glimmered in darkness. He walked around the shining wing of a great plane parked near the gate, climbed the steep stairs to his Constellation, and handed his gate pass to the waiting stewardess. Inside the plane, he looked ahead of him, and the idea of choosing an interesting companion dropped from his mind when he took in the fact that most of the double seats were empty. He sat down in the outside seat of the pair nearest the seats where the stewardesses would sit, and wondered. Something was wrong.

One late passenger came crashing up the steps and panted at the door, "Whew!" He stood there for a while, blowing out his breath hard, and then came ahead and found a seat. That made nine passengers in all. The pilot came aboard, exchanged a word or two with the two stewardesses at the door, and then went on up to the front of the plane, where the second pilot and the engineer already were. Then the stairs were wheeled away, an attendant outside made some laughing remark to the stewardesses, and the heavy door ground into place and the bolt turned. The engines roared, subsided, roared again, and the stewardesses came forward. Nine people in a plane made for sixty. It was eerie.

"May I take your coat?" one of the girls asked him. He glanced up at her. She looked like Loretta Young, with the same large, liquid eyes, the same heavy, shining lips and lovely white skin.

He handed her his raincoat and said, "Anybody up in the compartment?"

"No."

"What's the matter?"

"I don't know. This is awful."

"Saturday night?"

"It's never been like this," she said, and turned to the woman across the aisle. "Your coat?"

The woman broke into Italian, and the girl laughed quietly, helplessly. "Coat," she said, "coat," reaching out to touch the black coat the woman clutched suspiciously in her lap. Then she saw that the woman's safety belt was not fastened, and she bent over and fastened it for her. "Keep shut," she said, but she did not try to take the coat.

The plane began to move along its runway, and the stewardess moved to the passenger ahead of the Italian woman.

"Your coat?" she said again, and again she was answered in Italian. She laughed, and Henry laughed. There was, apparently, no connection between the two foreigners. The woman was in her sixties, a gaunt-looking peasant who twisted her harsh hands together in her lap; the man ahead of her was in his late thirties, an urban type, dressed in a thick tweed suit of a dogtooth pattern, black-and-white checks at least a half inch square. He laughed confidently up at the stewardess with a flash of white teeth in his dark face, and spoke again in Italian. She touched his coat, and he shrugged. She took it, and then glanced at Henry and smiled at him, and he leaned forward in his seat toward the ravishing generosity of her smile.

"It's crazy," he said to her. "Only nine people and two of them Italians who don't know each other."

The plane was ready for its takeoff, roaring at the end of the airstrip, and then began its race across the ground. The Italian woman groaned and clutched the arms of her seat. Loretta Young moved on, and the nearly empty plane lifted, a great empty metal shell rising in the blackness, and Henry imagined it for a moment light as a soap bubble or a dandelion fluff blowing along on the dark currents of the night, and when he leaned toward the round window at his left after a while and looked down and saw, almost directly below them, the maze of moving, twinkling, crazy lights that meant Palisades Park, and thought of the masses of people down there, jammed together on this Saturday night while he moved over them, unknown, almost alone in an enormous plane, he felt altogether separate from earth, from the familiar things he thought that he loved—felt positively unanchored. And that vague melancholy that he had pleasantly felt in the terminal bar, simply a sign that he was tired after three days of hard work, now seemed to pull itself together in his stomach and reach up inside him and clutch. He shook his head sharply in amazement.

The stewardess was speaking gently to the man who wore the absurd panama hat. The man had not removed the hat, and he declined now to let her put it on the rack over his head. He had seized the rim of the thing with both hands, and he was pulling it down over his ears, as though he thought she would try to remove it by force.

"But you'll be more comfortable, sir," she murmured. "You'll want to sleep."

"I can't sleep," he cried back at her in an oddly high-pitched voice.

She shrugged. "Very well," she said, and passed on.

"Jesus!" Henry said aloud. "Characters! All characters!" But his impatience drained away when the second stewardess came toward him with the seating chart. As he gave her his name, he was astonished to notice that she really looked a great deal like Bette Davis, with that same tensely neurotic beauty that he had always found so particularly exciting, and the scornful droop of the lips, too. She had, besides, short red hair, a charmingly slender waist, and trim legs rising out of neat, high-heeled pumps, and he gazed up at her with a kind of fatuous gratitude as she studiously wrote down his name, smiled at him briefly, and passed on behind him.

Now the lights in the cabin went out, and there was only a pinpoint ray from a reading light here and there cutting sharply through the droning darkness. The green FASTEN SEAT BELTS—NO SMOKING sign went out, too, and a few matches flared. Henry reached into his pocket and found a cigarette. Then the girls came forward again, offering blankets and pillows from the racks overhead, and the Italian woman tried to describe with her hands the sensation of her stomach, the lift and fall of nausea. The two girls wrapped her up in a blanket, and one brought a wet cloth and laid it over her forehead and the other placed a carton, suggestively open, in her lap. The woman groaned with soft dismay, and the girls returned to their seats again.

Then the plane seemed to move into a new zone of quiet. The engines seemed to burn down to an almost noiseless throb. Henry let his seat drop back, and from his half-reclining position he studied the tops of the several heads that jutted up over the seats in front of him, and he let his eyes rest finally on the panama hat, which was at once so eccentric and so pompous. More than ever then, with these few odd strangers in it, the plane seemed empty, and suddenly he remembered a flight he had made from New York to Boston during the war. In those years there was never an empty seat on a plane, and people queued up in airports all over America simply on the chance of a seat. There was a term—"No show," or "Go show," or something of the sort—that meant that if a passenger with a reservation did not turn up, you could go in his place. And late one afternoon when Henry was to fly up to Boston for one of those semiannual sales conferences from another of which he was now returning, a queer thing had happened. At flight time, one passenger had not appeared, and his seat was given to an elderly, plump, and prosperous-looking businessman who had been standing by for passage to Providence, where the plane made a landing. Then a delay occurred; five minutes passed, ten minutes; still the engines were quiet, and suddenly there was a hubbub of excited conversation outside the plane. Presently the stewardess came forward and spoke to the blue-suited, prosperous-looking man; the passenger whose seat he occupied had now arrived, and would he please give up the seat? The man's face went an apoplectic red under his well-brushed silvery hair. He would not indeed; if the departure had not been delayed, he would now be in the air, and he would certainly keep the seat. He tightened his safety belt and hung on to it pugnaciously.

The stewardess had spoken softly, but the blue-suited one simply stared stubbornly to the front. She shrugged and moved away. Then the two pilots appeared. They explained again, and after repeating his arguments for keeping the seat, the blue-suited one told them who he was. He was the president of a well-known watch company; it was imperative that he get to Providence, and not on his account but on account of the war effort; he did not know who the other passenger was, but he was sure the man's contribution was not as important as that of the watch company. The pilots were not impressed, and they pointed out that right then the watch company was holding up the flight and twenty-one legitimate passengers. They would have to call the police. Call the police, said the watch company.

By then, the passengers on the plane, who had at first been amused and then only mildly nettled, were angry. There were restrained mutterings and a buzzing of conversation, and one somewhat strident call from a sailor at the back of the plane: "Where's your priority, Big Shot?" Before the two policemen came on board, the engines started up, but the man seemed unperturbed; he stared ahead and sat stolidly in his seat, clutching at his safety belt.

"Sorry, sir, but you'll have to leave the plane," one of the police officers said to him.

"You'll have to put me off," he said.

"We'd hate to, but we can."

"Go ahead. Put me off forcibly."

The two officers looked at each other and shrugged, and the sailor shouted, "Put him off. I got only eight hours more of my liberty."

"That boy's being transferred to the Pacific, sir," the second police officer explained. "There's a wounded soldier on board who's being flown to a hospital for special treatment. Everybody has his own job to do, just like you."

"You'll have to put me off forcibly."

"O.K., mister," the first police officer said in a harder

voice, and reached forward to unfasten the man's safety belt.

"Wait a minute," the blue suit said. "First you'll give me your names and your numbers, and you can expect to hear of this. Remember that you're putting me off by force." He reached into his pocket and brought out a memorandum book and a pen.

The policemen looked at him and laughed. "Sure," they said together, and they recited their names and numbers. "Ready now?"

"Put me off."

They unfastened his seat belt and lifted him from his seat. Once he was in the aisle, he gave in. "Pick him up," called the sailor, but it was not necessary. The man went off the plane. And then the second man came on. He was a little man, a short, dark, cloak-and-suit type, middle-aged, and he looked embarrassed by the fuss he had caused. As the little man took his seat with a confused smile, the passengers began to clap and shout approval, and there was a general buzz of happy excitement, as if an important principle had been vindicated. Then the door was slammed, and the plane took off, and conversation between the passengers never stopped for the hour it took to get to Providence. There everyone laughed again, and when the little man got off, the sailor cheered.

Things were different then, Henry thought with sleepy nostalgia. There was a kind of excitement in the air then that drew people together and made them more human than they ordinarily were, and the contrast with his present situation, in effect alone on an empty plane made for sixty, saddened him and roused him from his sleepy state. Now it was harder to sell books, too, just as, apparently, it was harder to sell plane space. Things had changed. He lit a cigarette and listened to the engines humming, and stared down out of the round window at the transient yellow lights of a country town far below, and then at nothing at all.

The two stewardesses, behind him, had been talking together in low voices, and now one of them suddenly raised her voice in animation. The voice was not pleasant. It had a flat, chopped, nasal quality, a basic *yak yak yak* that meant Kansas or Nebraska, and no course in Oral Delivery at the State U., either. It could not be the Loretta one, with whom Henry had spoken; it must be the red-haired Bette Davis type, and it seemed strange that such an otherwise stylish girl should not have caught on about her voice. She was telling the other girl some story, full of "then he"s and "then she"s, and the voice chopped on in an almost pitiless way—*yak yak yak*—in the darkness.

The very contrast reminded Henry of the new promotion woman in the office, that cool Boston type with the beautifully clipped speech, a really smart voice that spoke of the Winsor School and childhood summers at Prides Crossing, and a four-story house on Beacon Hill with a big library and a music room, and summer evenings in a white chiffon gown on the Ritz roof. Henry was growing sleepy again, and as he put out his cigarette, he was almost able to substitute that charming voice for the one that went on behind him. Miss Priscilla Thayer was the name. She was a handsome girl in her early thirties, with short black hair and a proud, boyish figure in a black gabardine suit, and a touch of bluntness in her manner, a little like—well, yes, a little like Katharine Hepburn. She had practically taken over the conference; Jim Moore, the top editor, had really turned it over to her, and there was no doubt that she had some fine, bright new ideas. Her theory was that every book had its own class audience—not just the "special" books, but every book, novels as well as cookbooks—and she had laid out the next two seasons in that way, tying in with each book the special groups among whom it should be promoted. On the first of those three days in the big room in the Parker House, some of the fellows had given this girl a very fishy eye; they were going to make her prove herself. Henry himself had had no doubts even at the beginning. She was a girl who knew how to handle herself, and when Henry asked her to go out with him on the second night, she turned him down so prettily that he could hardly feel that he had been turned down. The suspicious fellows were won over, too, as the smoke grew thicker in the room, and the sandwiches got to seem staler, and the joint hangover each morning was harder to shake. She even managed, somehow, to take the shock off the news in the papers on the third morning, when they all read that their brightest young best-selling novelist had drowned in an inexplicable accident at sea, somewhere off the coast of Florida.

The voices behind Henry had softened down. The girls were talking still, but very quietly now. There was no light on in the plane, and no sound except their subdued voices and an occasional soft sigh from the Italian woman across from Henry. He felt sleep working through him like the gentle droning that came from the engines and as he closed his eyes, he was wondering in an idle way why two such lovely girls as those behind him should be unmarried —such clear-eyed, trim, beautiful girls, and no husbands— with successful young guys jumping off boats out at sea, and Fifth Avenue full of bouncing pansies, and pansies lined up three deep at the Pine Room bar, where he used to like to stop for a beer. "Things fall apart; the center cannot hold," he quoted dreamily to himself from a poem in an anthology that he handled. Such handsome girls going begging. His head sank slowly.

Then he was selling books. He was talking fast, and at first he did not realize that he was talking to no one, but he was giving out that new sales line, and he thought he was doing all right, until suddenly he was aware that he was in an empty airplane, a completely empty airplane; there were not even any pilots. In what should have been the pilots' cabin, there were the usual crowded instrument panels but nothing else; the instruments were working away busily, with needles moving back and forth across dials, and lights blinking red and green, and the plane was flying high and steadily—pure machine, completely under control. But Henry, facing the empty seats and then lurching up and down the aisle as he sought for just one live customer hiding somewhere, grew miserable. He kept on talking anyway, selling, selling—something for Granny, something light and humorous; something for the Busy Housewife, something hot, something historical; something for Junior; something for the Concerned Executive; something for Aunt Polly, a work on cooking and gardening and embroidery, all in one, with a little religion, not heavy; and something, too, for the kiddies; and this special something for the subdeb daughter who wants to learn how to make up that soft, woundable mouth; and for that boy home from the service who just committed suicide, there is the special —Oh, *Jesus!*

Henry groaned in his misery as he lurched through the empty plane, addressing the empty seats, but then everything seemed to change again, and he realized suddenly that he had not really had a fix on the situation at all, that all these seats were really to be taken, and taken right away, because here were two for Jennifer and Betty, here two for blond Ingrid and dark Barbara, here were two more for Ginger and Rita, here were two for Paulette and Marlene, and here for Greta and gorgeous Joan, and here for Loretta and—and her friend, whose name escaped him. The whole plane was to be filled with these lovely girls, and he was to go around and sell his books to *them,* and for a moment he went way up into a cloudland of exhilaration, into a kind of crazy, drunken, lifting happiness, and then a voice broke in on him—*yak yak yak*—and he jerked to pull himself up out of that sleep.

Henry was sitting up in the dark, nearly empty plane, still struggling out of his loose sleep, and as he came into wakefulness, an idea was present in his mind, as if it had been waiting there for him to rouse himself sufficiently to take it in in all its shattering clarity: *A machine is a lonely thing.*

As the thought struck him, the back of his neck went cold, went all goose flesh, as it had when he first heard that colored girl sing those words, "My lips, my love," only now, besides, he could feel the clipped hair on the back of his neck positively rise, as if, with this simple thought, he had seen a ghost or had a revelation from God, and he shuddered.

Then the clarity of the thought blurred in his mind, and the prickly sensation on the back of his neck subsided, and sitting up straight, he saw ahead of him the tops of those isolate heads, one of them with the hat still upon it, all rigid in their uncomfortable loneliness, locked in the prisons of their useless languages, their intractable solitude, in the great oval metal belly of the plane, and then the voice of the Bette Davis type behind him broke on his ears again—*yak yak yak*, pure Nebraska—and in a weary way he reached up and pressed the button over his head.

A chime struck out dimly in the nearly empty Constellation. Then Loretta Young appeared beside him. He lay back, gazing up into her great liquid eyes. He said, "Look, tell Bette to pipe down. Tell her to come sit here." He patted the empty seat beside him. "I'll keep her quiet."

"What did you say, sir?"

He looked up at the loose, lovely mouth. "Oh, my God!" he said, and then, for reasons that he did not know and could not possibly have known, he felt his throat

tighten. And the four droning engines, which he had become aware of again in his still-sleepy state, were now as-
suredly his own feelings—they were his sadness; they were
his awful, empty sorrow—and out of his lingering dream
he began really to cry, round tears rolling down over his
plump, substantial cheeks, and said, "Get me, please, a
drink of water."

FRANK

*T*he connection with my grandparents' house remained close. I have no recollection of either of those old people coming over to our house (although they must have), but I remember always going over to theirs. On one day a week my grandmother made waffles, and either my brother or I would be sent over to bring a stack of waffles to our house, our supper. We were regularly sent over there to help old Jaeger with his household chores. He had a large lawn that required mowing, and we would push the lawnmower back and forth under his rather imperious direction. He ordered large amounts of wood that needed to be split for the stoves, and while he split, seated on a stump before another stump, we would pile the wood. Once, I remember, a pig was butchered in the back yard, between the henhouse and the stable, and a good deal of very messy disemboweling, bloodletting, chopping up of parts, and so on followed, the meat to be salted down for the winter. This must have happened rather regularly, once a year. I remember loathing the sausages that he made, flushing out and cutting up the veritable entrails of the beast and then stuffing them. *Blutwurst!*

My friend Frank lived near my grandparents' house. He was a little younger than I and I can't remember when we really became close friends. I thought of him, I think, as rather strange. He was given to "running away from home," which is to say, wandering off from the family property, and his mother would then search the streets, find him, bring him home, and tie him up to a clothesline post with a piece of clothesline, six or eight feet, like a small animal. I would go over there and just stare at him, tied up.

His sister, Evelyn, was six or seven years older than we were, and when I was eight years old, one day when both Frank and his mother were gone, she got me up on her parents' bed and took down my pants and stuffed my little limp wiener of a penis into her vulva. "What is this called?" I asked, and, "Fucking," said she. There was a strange odor. I had no sensation at all, only wonder. Another time she tried this with me on the piano bench, heaven knows why. And a third time in the privy outside, when we were playing hide-and-seek with Frank. But presently, it was generally whispered about, she was really screwing boys more nearly her own age, and I remember one night, in the orchard that they owned, watching her silhouette and that of a high-school senior and athlete named "Doc" Byers (his father was a dentist, hence the nickname). This must have been in about 1922, when I was a freshman in high school, for I had observed "Doc" naked in the locker room, an observation that bore out his reputation as being the most generously endowed boy (man?) in the school. At any rate, hiding behind some shrubbery, I saw by the dim light of street lamps how he had backed her up against an apple tree and was fucking her presumably to her satisfaction. For some reason I felt ruined.

By this time the friendship between Frank and me was fading. As we moved into our adolescence, he became increasingly involved in sports, I in books, and the difference seemed to mean a drifting apart. A more congenial friendship developed with a very witty boy named Karl, slick and easy with a dry or sometimes cruel riposte, a great one-liner. He could have become a fine stand-up comic, writing his own scripts, but I don't suppose that stand-up comics existed then except possibly in some primitive vaudeville version. At any rate, Karl elected to become a very good school teacher of German and English, no doubt endlessly entertaining to and sharply critical of his pupils.

When we began to tipple in high school, he was, as he would be later, my drinking companion, and if I lived in Wisconsin today, he would still be that, the most amusing, the most tolerant, the best of men.

A N O T H E R

C O U N T R Y

Lunch would not be served for another hour, but the impossible Greek boy, Nello, who wolfed his food in a disgusting way, was already waiting for it. He was playing his guitar and singing, sitting on a stool in a low arbor where enormous bunches of green grapes nearly touched his hair. How she despised him! She was fourteen and full of fury. She had just started a letter to her best friend in the *Stati Uniti* (as *they* said) and she had written the following: "Dear Mary— Why does this have to happen to me? The crossing was fun, there was a swimming pool and lots of Americans, but here there aren't any but us and I hate it. I mean here in this house." Then she had stopped writing to listen impatiently to the outrageous Greek boy, Nello, they called him, and she said with quiet rage but almost hoping that he would hear her, "*Mi non piacere.*" Her Italian had not advanced beyond infinitives.

Her name was Suzanne, but they all insisted on calling her Susanna, so unfamiliar in its sound that half the time when they addressed her she did not respond at all, simply not knowing. Susan-*na!* How she hated that! And then a whole string of words came after her name, with little moans and groans: *carina, carinissima, bellina, biondissima!* And then they almost always made it worse by doing that outrageous thing that Italians do to children to show, she guessed, affection: they would seize a piece of her cheek between the knuckles of their first two fingers and pinch and pull and even twist. When Nello did that, she could spit at him, or die! Ye gods! she exclaimed to herself, and impatiently shifted her position on the broad beige marble steps that led from the dining room into the garden. She wrote that phrase in her letter: "Ye gods!" and continued: "We are living in what's called a *pensione.* The city is Perugia, it's in the province of Umbria." Then she put both the pen and pad on the steps beside her, and, her elbows on her naked knees, she propped her chin in her hands and stared out at as much of Umbria as she could see. Nello's Greek song grew distant in her ears, and since she was not now looking at him, not even at the back of his abominable head with all that hair, things did not seem quite so bad and her little rage began to subside.

Signora Pacetti's house was new and stood outside the old walls. Up above it the cluttered gray city labored to its peak, but below it the country began at once, first falling steeply away through orchards to a stream, then rising and falling gently through miles of golden October mist: gray-green olive groves, tidily terraced fields of brown and green and yellow, and nearly chartreuse vineyards clinging to the hillsides. But over all these patterns and colors lay the golden air. She saw it now whenever the sun shone, ever since a recent Sunday when a guide in the municipal museum had explained to Suzanne and her mother that if you could not recognize a landscape by Perugino in any other way, there were always two marks to identify him: the Lago

Trasimeno would be somewhere in the picture, probably in the middle distance, and the overall tone would be golden, "our Umbrian gold." She sighed as she stared out at the country, and she drifted into a mindless reverie from which only the voices of her parents, coming from the balcony off their bedroom directly above the steps where she sat, at last aroused her.

"I wonder what the ulcer rate is here," her father was saying vigorously, as though he were making an announcement.

"Nonexistent, I'm sure," her mother answered, "but they have liver trouble instead."

"That's diet, not nerves."

She waited for more words from the low balcony, but none came. She knew exactly what they were doing and how they looked: they were sitting in deck chairs with two glasses and a flagon of Orvieto wine on a round table between them; they were both wearing their new Italian sunglasses, and each held a book (Suzanne could give their titles if she were asked) in which they read a little between sips. Presently they would exchange a few short sentences again, but for the moment, nothing. Even Nello had stopped singing, his fingers plucking softly and infrequently on his strings as they aimlessly searched for another tune, and all one really heard was the warm buzz of noon, as if the sunlight itself had the voice of bees.

She leaned back on the steps and lifted her face to the sun, and now she was as content as a cat. She wondered vaguely which sounds would break this spell—the neutral voices of her parents, the mocking wail of another of Nello's songs, or, worst of all, the shrill scream of the signora as she called to her wretched maid—"Marissa!"

Noontime murmured on, and into that vague hum Nello's plucked notes thudded softly and were absorbed, like stones falling into a deep well. Then there was an abrupt little skirmish of sound and his voice started up again, the incomprehensible Greek words gurgling lavishly in his throat. She looked toward him and she saw that he had turned on his stool and was facing her, leering as he sang. Instinctively she tried to cover her legs, but she was wearing shorts, very brief young-American-girl shorts, and she could not. Her own gesture outraged her. She knew that her face was burning red, and she straightened up indignantly, seized her pen and pad, and began to write with angry purpose.

In rapid strokes, her careful back slant disappeared as she told her friend about the inhabitants of the *pensione*. There were the signora and her two silent sons, who were studying to be doctors and whose father had been killed in Africa in the war. There was an old judge with a white beard whom everyone called "Commendatore," which was a kind of title. There was a "doctor" from Amalfi who was really an engineer working on some project for the city and whose thick Neapolitanese she was completely unable to understand even as she was beginning to understand the others. There were two mousy Swiss girls who studied at the university and spoke about six languages. They all sat at one long table.

Oh, and there were two Greek boys studying to be veterinarians, about eighteen years old, one an outrageous creature named Nello with yellowish, crowded teeth and masses of tightly crinkled hair that came right down around his ears and down into his collar on the back of his neck, and who, before he would let her begin her food, always made her give the Italian words for table objects he held up or pointed to. "*Susanna! Come si chiama, questa?*" And then: *la forchetta, il coltello, il cucchiaio, il piatto, il tovagliolo, il bicchiere, la caraffa, il vino, l'acqua, il sale, il pepe, il pane;* the whole long series at every meal, and always leering, while her parents sat on either side of her smiling their approval.

"Really, Mary," she wrote, "if it weren't for this great

oaf, I'd have a chance to enjoy Italy. There is much to enjoy. The country is lovely even though the people are very poor, or most of them—strange and different and often inconvenient, but exciting. Oh, well, we have only three more weeks in this house, then we have an apartment in Florence—" She looked at the last word she had written, crossed it out, and wrote "Firenze" instead, and added, "—for the winter, and I'll be in school again, although a different one from ours."

Her father was a classicist with an archaeological interest, at work on an Etruscan project, and he was spending his first five weeks in the Etrusco-Roman Museum in Perugia. Then he would have to move about to many places, but she and her mother would settle in Florence for the winter. Nello's song thumped to a stop, and when she permitted herself to glance in his direction, she saw that the stool was empty, the guitar with its purple ribbon leaning against it, and Nello deep in the arbor, wolfing a bunch of grapes. She turned sharply away. In Florence she would not ever have to think of *him* again, she consoled herself, and started when, at that moment, she heard her mother's sharp laughter above her. It was almost as if her mother knew what was in her mind, for with that same laugh she had on several occasions in the past few weeks dismissed Suzanne's expressed distaste for Nello. But now the laughter was in fact about something quite different.

"What is it?" her father asked in his clear, metallic voice.

"I like this. It's very nice."

"I've warned you that one can't take that book seriously."

"Perhaps not. But this is very nice."

Yes, Suzanne said to herself, the paper-covered book, *Etruscan Places*.

"A lot of Lawrentian nonsense," he said firmly but

mildly, and then Suzanne let herself miss a brief interchange as she speculated on the fact that it was precisely
such a difference of opinion as this which, a year ago, even
two months ago, would have had them quarreling. They
never quarreled any more. For a year, perhaps two years,
there had been some kind of struggle going on; then suddenly they had declared an armistice. They were always
mild and polite now, as if, in another country, something
had happened to them, but she thought that she preferred
them as they were before, even when, night after night at
the dinner table, there would be sharp little disagreements
if there were not actual scenes. Now it was as if they were
unentangled, as if they had gone away from one another.
Her father kept his clear, stentorian tone of voice, a kind of
public voice, but the anger that used to swell it was gone; it
was like a shell, just an old habit that hung on. And her
mother's voice never rose to shrillness any more; it became
only more secretive, and was given to saying more and more
mysterious things. It was saying them now.

"Which passage? This, about how they planned their
cemeteries. On one hill the living city; on another hill opposite, at which they could look, the city of the dead. It's
such a forthright view."

"In fact, of course, untrue."

"Perhaps. But if it's untrue, I'm sorry. I can believe
they were that way. We should be."

"How?" her father asked.

"How? Always know which city we're in. Not think
we're in the living city when we're really in the shadow
city."

"When you say 'we,' whom do you mean?"

"I'm not, dear Will, talking about civilizations."

"I didn't think so, but it's still untrue. There are no
such sharp lines in the realities of personality, either. We're
always crossing back and forth. Things change. They will

again. I think I will, if you'll help a little. I'm not fifty yet."

"*Speriamo!*" she cried out almost derisively. "I'm not yet forty!" And her father did not answer.

Suzanne hugged her sides. If only he went on now, or if only her mother would say something more! She felt that she was on the very edge of understanding something; they were almost, for a change, making sense to her! But they were silent, and the more she strained to hear, the more firm their silence seemed to grow, as if not only their words but their very selves had disappeared into the noontide hum. Not words, but slow steps on the gravel roused her from her strained intentness. She turned quickly and saw Nello approaching, his guitar under his arm, his shoulders swaying. He was wearing a red-and-white-striped shirt and silly, tight cotton trousers. She made herself relax.

"*Come stai, Susanna?*" he asked quietly as he slouched down beside her, smiling his yellow smile and gently putting his guitar down.

"*Non c'e male,*" she said doggedly, hating him, repeating one of the phrases he had made her learn.

He looked intently into the still darkened dining room as if to make sure that no one was there, and then he said tauntingly, softly, "*Carina.*"

She shrugged her shoulders, tossing off the word, and turned away from him as she saw his hand lift. Now would come that damned cheek pinching! She grew rigid in preparation. But something else happened. One arm slid softly behind her shoulders, and the other hand did not pinch her, but, palm open, laid itself coarsely on her cheek. "*Bellina,*" the throaty voice murmured in her ear, and her stiffness turned to a shudder. The rough hand stroked her face and she could not move, she could not cry out, she could not look. Her eyes were clamped shut. Terror held her. The hand moved down to her neck. She felt his breath on her face like a hot, sluggish wind. She tried to scream, but she only moaned. The hand slid to her small breast. "*Carissima*," the voice whispered, and she shook violently in the hot sunlight under the hand on her breast.

Then abruptly, somewhere in the house, the signora screamed, "*Marissa! Il tavolo!*" Only that, but the air-splitting command made Nello leap away from her like a frightened animal. Before Suzanne had opened her eyes, he had snatched up his ribboned guitar and fled. Then instantly she seized her pen and paper and ran, too. She ran into the grape arbor and, so that she would be out of her parents' sight, around the side of the house. Under a peach tree was a wooden bench. She sat down on this abruptly, as if hands had pushed her on it. She could not stop trembling, even as, once more, she felt her familiar rage, but heightened now, and felt her face red hot with her indignant blushing. She gripped the edge of the seat in an effort to control her body, and slowly her shaking stopped. Then, preparing to gather herself together and go to her room, she looked at the pad in her lap and read her half-finished letter. She tore the sheet from the pad, crumpled it into a ball, held it a moment, and tossed it under the bush that, all pompously groomed, rounded and waiting, seemed to expect such a letter as it stood beside her. Then, looking out at the field and hills and vineyards across the valley, foolish tears that she could not stop rose to her eyes, but she kept her eyes open and tried hard and in vain to keep that landscape clear, to keep it from dissolving into the golden blur that it already was.

PAY-OFF

*A*t La Toque Blanche not long ago the waiter recommended the lapin, and the suggestion brought back in a flash recollections of my father as hunter, or rather, of the game that he brought back from his frequent excursions into the woods and fields, rabbits and squirrels and doves. These my mother would cook and serve. I remember picking the fragments of buckshot out of my mouth. I did not order the lapin.

Once, thinking that he had sighted a goose flying over our house, he shot the creature and it came hurtling down out of the sky, a great white swan, its wings beating the ground, its long neck still writhing. Since there was a heavy state penalty for killing swans, there was much secretive excitement over quickly getting the dying bird into the house. It was roasted, as if indeed it were a goose. And at least once my father shot a raccoon, and we ate that, too. I have no recollection of the taste, only that for a long time the pelt was nailed up on the inside of the garage door.

My grandfather was a fisherman rather than a hunter. When he was old and rheumatic and I was ten or eleven, he used to pay me five cents to haul him down to the river in my coaster wagon. He would sit on the back and shove the wagon along with thrusts of his stick while I pulled. He liked to fish from a bank at a spot below the creamery, about six blocks away from his house. I felt only chagrin as I pulled the old man down the street for that wretched bribe of a nickel, when in fact I had no choice. My father was always determined that the old man must be satisfied in all his unreasonable whims, as they seemed to me. There was that thought of a fortune, and much irritation when, after the First World War, he began to send money to his impoverished relatives in Germany; but no abatement in the effort to please him.

Sauk City sent two young men to that war and one of them was killed. Most of the citizenry was vigorously patriotic, but some of the older residents, with their closer relation to what was called "the old country," were secretly sympathetic to the enemy. My grandfather was openly sympathetic and vociferous about it, a "pro-German," and during one night the sides of his house, which was white, were daubed with broad streaks of yellow paint, resulting in a hasty effort next morning by my father to cover them with white.

In 1929 I had reason to recall those embarrassing five-cent coaster-wagon excursions. I was about to graduate from the University of Wisconsin, and having decided to become a teacher, I wanted very much to attend graduate school at Harvard for at least a year. From Madison I wrote my grandfather a letter in German—*Lieber Grossvater!*—asking if he could give me $2,500 to see me through such a year. I explained what a graduate school was, how professionally advantageous it would be if I had at least an M.A. from Harvard, and how after that I would return to the University of Wisconsin for the Ph.D. With the Harvard M.A., I could almost certainly obtain a teaching assistantship at Wisconsin and would be able to carry myself. None of this could have made much sense to him but, without asking me any questions, he said that he would give me the money. The coaster wagon had paid off! Or the fact that I had written him in German. Or both.

What remains more vividly with me than anything that happened during that year in Cambridge is the image of that old man, after one of our detestable fishing excursions, digging into his pocket and hauling out his leather coin purse, from which he would studiously extract my wage, embossed with its buffalo.

A BURNING

GARDEN

The yellow acacia blossoms of the spring hung in heavy pods on the moping trees, and the roses, which had bloomed enormous and odorless, rotted on their stems like neglected vegetables in the mists and fogs of California summer. The yucca had shot up a great obscene arm, twenty, thirty feet into the air, a horrid, disproportionate tube that had dangled tassel flowers and dropped seeds and then started to brown and shrivel, and now, they said, the plant had run its life and it would die. Young Mrs. Fairbank stood in her garden and began to sob.

But—garden? Well, hardly. All right, call it a non-garden then, her neighbor might have said. Why was she sobbing there in her non-garden, sitting now in a crushed heap on the overgrown flagstones, her face buried in the gingham of her skirt and her tossed brown hair? Why, indeed? some resilient part of Mrs. Fairbank could still demand. She threw up her head and looked around her with a queer, probing motion, like a blind creature out of the earth, feeling its way with the front of its body, its head.

The shape of her laundry basket came in a yellow blur through her flooded sight, and when she saw it for what it was, she wiped her eyes with the edge of her skirt and stood up as briskly as she could.

She stood in thin, misty light that was neither warm nor cold. She looked past the blackened side of the old redwood cottage that was her rented home, looked down over the luxuriant tops of eucalyptus and live oak, over the neutral flats of roofs, looked across the wide expanse of gray bay to the city beyond, piled up on its brow of peninsula, its gray towers piercing through the white fog that still, at mid-morning, bound its streets. Cool and distant, it seemed, from where she stood, an uninhabited dream of a silver city in clouds, fabled, inhuman. Once more, tears leaped to her eyes, so that she said, "Damn, damn!" and bent resolutely to her laundry basket. But when in doing so her dimmed eye crept over that shriveling upthrust of the yucca, she felt suddenly dizzy with sickness, so overpowering was the sensation she had of being trapped there, with that *thing!*

She craved with a fierce melancholy, now as almost always, an image of her relinquished past: a New Hampshire snowfield that lay behind a village church and parish house, a field marked off by low gray stone walls shelved with snow, empty except for a half dozen apple trees naked of leaves, their branches an anatomy of the full round of summer; beside the church a graveyard as old as the village, crowded with the anonymous, weather-worn symbols of old, nearly inconceivable death, snow piled softly between them, a few pines rising lordly above; the church spire plain and geometric, white against gray sky; and in the rectory, her home, the first lights of winter evening gilding the banked snow under the windows from which they shone. A worn, frustrating question always followed upon this recollection—What am I doing here?—and it followed now as she began to pin up her laundry. Diapers, tea towels, little undershirts, diapers, socks, little sweater. Then, "Good morning," a familiar voice heartily sang out.

Helen Fairbank turned to see her neighbor Brenda White pushing her way through a gap in the tall, ill-kept privet hedge that stood uncertainly between their nearly identical houses. She was the plump, childless wife of the manager of a Safeway store, and this morning she was wearing scuffed red flats, green corduroy slacks, a shapeless pink cardigan, and, tied around her head, a white scarf printed with horses. A cigarette was in her mouth and a pair of garden shears in her hand. "How's my boy?" she asked, the cigarette bobbing.

Helen Fairbank took a clothespin from between her teeth. "Which one?"

"Either one. I was thinking of Bill. Didn't he take an examination or something this morning? But how's the little one? He's my boy, too. You been crying, honey?"

Helen stared at her and asked blankly, "What am I doing here?"

Mrs. White's fifty-year-old face broke into wrinkles and seemed to smile all over. "Well, for one thing, honey, it's your home," she said cheerfully, with a brief, raucous laugh. She dropped her cigarette on a flagstone and ground it out with her sandal, and she put her shears down beside a chair. "Tell Brenda," she said, coming closer, and then bent to pick a diaper from the basket, shake it out, and fix it to the clothesline. "Sit down. I'll finish this," she said.

"I can do it."

They did it together, and for a moment the sun, almost breaking through the high mist, shone warm upon them, but when all the laundry had been hung, the sky had reverted to its neutral blur, and in this thin gray light they sat down together on faded canvas deck chairs that had once been gaudy.

"Tell Brenda," Mrs. White said again.

"I don't really *know*," Helen said with a desperate emphasis. "Only—I'm so—so—"

"So what?"

Helen's thoughtful, unhappy face was lifted. She stared down at the distant bay, where, on the glassy gray surface of the water, a boat had appeared and was pouring smoke into the air. "Is that boat burning?" she asked.

Mrs. White glanced away, and for a moment the loose flesh on her neck tautened as she craned to see. "No, no."

"But all that smoke."

"It's nothing. It's getting ready to refuel, or something. Tell me what you're sick of."

"Day in, day out. This is no kind of life. We have no money. We can't ever do anything. Day after day I'm stuck here, in this house, with nothing to do but the same stupid things. For nearly three years now." All this she said quietly, and then, "I have *nothing!*" she suddenly wailed.

With a fingernail the size of an almond and the color of garnets, Brenda White traced the grooves of corduroy stretched tight across her heavy knee. "You have the baby. You have your husband. What do you think being married is?"

Helen shivered and, wrapping her arms together, bent forward a little, as with a cramp.

"Where's Bill? Is he here?"

"No, no. He's taking that Latin."

"Doesn't seem like him. Latin."

Helen glanced at her quickly. "And why not?"

"Maybe you should have left him where he was. Teaching high school in that small town. Sounds comfortable. And coaching basketball. That's more for him than Latin. What did he teach? History and Spanish? But easy history and Spanish. He looks tired. It's a strain. Does everybody have to have a Ph.D.? Maybe you should have let it ride."

"I?" Helen cried. "*I*? That's silly. It was only sensible. He had three years of G.I. money coming, he'll improve his position immensely—"

"Well, then," Mrs. White broke in, "why are you complaining? He's nearly finished now, and—"

"I said—I don't really *know!* I just—well, I hate *this!*" and she flung her bare brown arms out to indicate the garden, the overgrown vegetation, the sodden flowers, the heavy trees. "This wretched parody of a summer!" She paused, and then, pointing to the yucca, said with soft intensity, "Look at that."

Brenda White apparently saw nothing. Hunting for a cigarette in the pockets of her slacks, she said, "It's a strain on him—the studying, I mean."

Helen spoke in quick defense. "I didn't let him cram yesterday. I made him relax. We went to the beach."

"Was that good? He told me Saturday he didn't know the stuff."

"Everyone knows that cramming at the end doesn't help."

"Oh."

"At the end, you should relax, if you can."

"Oh."

"We went to the beach. We brought back a bird."

"A bird?"

"A cormorant."

"What for?"

"It couldn't fly. We were sitting on the sand, watching a lot of birds, and when they all flew away, this one was left, sitting on the water, and finally a swell carried it right in to the shore, high up on the sand, and left it sitting there helplessly, very near us. It sat there, looking at us and then out to sea again. It couldn't move. When we went closer, it hissed at us, but Bill picked it up and we found that its whole breast and its feet were covered with tar. So we put it in a box and brought it home. I'm trying to clean the tar off, and then we'll take it back."

Brenda White looked at her with open curiosity and said, "You're out of breath, honey."

Helen's lips were parted, her head was lifted, and her eyes, bright and wide, seemed to rest again on the distant city.

"What's so special about that bird?"

She started a little and said, "Special? Nothing. But it is rather extraordinary. I'll get it!" And she rose at once and hurried over to the flagstone steps that ran uncertainly down the side of the bank between the terrace and the house below it. She disappeared into the basement by a side door, but reappeared in a moment, smiling, carrying a paper carton under one arm and, in the hand of the other, a bowl and a roll of cotton wrapped in blue paper. These she set carefully at Mrs. White's feet and then knelt on a flat stone beside them. Carefully, even cautiously, she opened the box.

The bird, crouched at the bottom of the box and tipped slightly against its side, as if for support, did not stir, but when Helen put one hand firmly on its gray back, the other gently on its long neck, it twisted its dark head upward and uttered a soft, dispirited hiss. Its unblinking eyes were coral red. It did not struggle in her hands as she lifted it from the box, and when she pushed it gently onto its side on her lap, it lay quietly and seemed relaxed, its undulant neck stretched out along her thigh. She examined its wings, then picked up its gnarled, webbed feet, and then she exposed to Brenda its breast, once white, coated with tar. Touching the tar, she could feel the bird's heart beating, and she said, "Yesterday there was a whole mass of this tar here. I've got a lot of it off."

"It's like a snake," Brenda said, peering down at the bird with distaste, her mouth a sour pucker.

"Poor fellow," Helen murmured as she reached for the cotton beside her.

"Are its eyes supposed to be that color?"

"I don't know. Hold this roll, will you, Brenda, so I can pull off a piece?"

"Those eyes—the thing must be sick!"

"That's the way they were yesterday. No, I'm sure it's just this tar." She dipped a piece of cotton in the bowl of kerosene and began gently to rub the cotton against the bird's breast feathers. The piece of soaked cotton came away black, but the tar on the matted feathers did not seem to lessen, even though Helen rubbed and rubbed, soaking the feathers around the tar, and frequently taking up a new piece of cotton and dipping it constantly in the now murky kerosene. She could feel the bird's long neck pressed softly against her leg, its quiet body resting warm in her lap, and she crooned to the creature as she rubbed, while Brenda White stared at her with her short, round chin resting reflectively in her hand.

"Well," Brenda said finally, and abruptly, picking up her shears, "this isn't getting my winter iris separated, is it?"

Helen just glanced at her and continued to attend to the bird. It had suddenly opened its long, hooked beak, so beautifully delicate, in what seemed to be an exquisite and comfortable yawn, and then let the two parts come slowly together again. Mrs. White was standing.

"When's Bill due home?"

"The exam's only an hour. He should be along." She stopped rubbing and studied the bird. "That's probably enough for now. I've been doing this since yesterday, every few hours. I think it's cleaner, don't you?"

Brenda stared at the recumbent bird. "I can't tell. Let me know how the Latin went." She ducked her head a little as she crowded her matronly shape through the hedge.

"Poor darling," Helen murmured to the bird as it slowly yawned again, and then she picked it up in her two hands and put it tenderly back in its box. She closed the flaps of the cover securely, took the box to the side of the terrace where no one would stumble over it, and then looked up into the sky for the sun. It was a faint, edgeless, dead-looking globe, and, through that high fog, looked more like the moon than the sun. It made no shadow in the garden, and overblown roses, rotting zinnias, grass and crabgrass, dripping pods and the great yucca growth—all were just themselves, fecund, fetid, and unqualified by light in the damp, dim air. Helen's picture of the plain snowfield, all grays and white, light and shadow, came sharply back to her mind, and with it, she wrapped her arms together again and sat down in one of the deck chairs in a torpor of sorrow, even as she heard the baby's cries coming from the dim interior of the house, even as she was dimly aware of doors opening and closing and feet on the floor.

"The baby was crying. Can't you hear him up here? I changed him," Bill's voice was saying presently, and she forced her dead stare to move from the distant city and to look toward him. Sunlight shone upon him. He was coming up the steps at the edge of the bank, pulling his T-shirt over his head as he came, and he stood beside her chair presently, looking down at her. "Are you sick?"

"No. How was the Latin?"

He balled up his shirt and threw it vigorously into the pouchy seat of the chair next to hers. "Three passages. Livy, Horace, Ovid. I couldn't even get started with the Ovid."

Something warmed her skin, perhaps the spreading sunlight. "You failed?"

"But good," he said, and kicked a stone with a thick-soled brown shoe.

"Oh, God! and now?"

"Now? I can't take it again for another semester. It puts everything off by that much."

She stood up. She stared at him. The sun shone in his light-brown hair, which was cut short, bristly, and square, so that his head had a blunt, aggressive quality. This haircut seemed to her well suited to the cut of his jaw, which thrust forward in a stubborn way, as if to defy her.

"I need the time to beat that Ovid."

His brown shoulders and chest seemed heavier and larger than they ever had, and they made her feel smaller than she was. His cotton khaki trousers hung rather low on his hips, so that the white top of his shorts showed above the top of his trousers, and now she looked at the uneven line of hair that straggled up to his navel. The sun gleamed in this, too.

"I'll whip it next time, don't worry."

She turned away from him and looked down to the water. There the boat was still burning. It could not really be burning or it would by now have been burned to nothing; but it was still pouring smoke into the brightening air. Across the bay the city stood out clear and beautiful, the fog gone, white buildings shining in sunlight against the blue Pacific sky.

She said tensely, "I can't stand an extra four months of this. I was counting on your taking your degree in February. How can we live? Your money will be gone."

"We'll manage."

"How?"

"We will, don't worry."

"I *won't* worry! I just won't do it at all."

"What will you do? There's nothing else. We have to stick it out now."

"No, not I."

"But look—"

"I *am* looking."

"Well?"

She heard a chair creak behind her, and when she turned around again, she saw him sprawled in one of the chairs, sitting on his shirt. His arms were lifted, hands behind his head, hair in a tangle in his armpits, legs flung out before him, and he lay in the thin sunlight as if in a pure dream of physical comfort.

"You *can't* be as content as you look!"

"I'm not content," he said quietly.

"Well? What *are* we going to do?"

"We'll manage. I can get that night job, assisting the coach at the city Y. I can get my father to help a little, for those few months. We can manage."

"But still eking out! Only even more so!"

"Has it been so bad?"

She stared at him again, at his body. His waist was not at all fat, but it was thick, and solid, and now, in his reclining position, his muscular stomach was thrust grossly out, as if to insult her. Impatiently she tossed her head. The fog was thinning, the sun was growing warmer, but she was cold. She wanted, once more, to cry.

"That the bird?" he asked, indicating the carton. "How is it?"

She answered, "Mrs. White wants to know about the Latin. She dotes on you."

He ignored what seemed to be her irrelevance. "How's the bird?"

She had felt, ever since he had told her about the examination, helpless, without an aim, without a possibility of action or even of open anger, and to rid herself of these feelings, she went purposefully to the box. She opened the covers slowly and put her hand inside to take out the resting bird, but this time it did not stir under her hand. Then, as she saw it plainly, she drew her hand sharply away. The bird lay limp and still in the box, its neck grotesquely twisted, its fragile beak stretched wide.

"Oh, no!" she cried

"What?"

"It's—oh, no! Not when I was just managing!"

Bill stood over her. "Dead?"

She had been kneeling. Now she sank abruptly down on her legs beside the box, and she looked up at him with blinded eyes in a stricken face.

"It must've been sick," he said, and moved awkwardly above her.

"It wasn't sick," she said. "It seemed well, it even seemed friendly."

"Weak, more likely." He sniffed the strong smell that rose from the box. "Maybe it was the kerosene. Did you put any air holes in that box?" He bent down to see.

"Oh, no!" Her words were a groan. "You don't think I—"

He straightened up at once. "No, it couldn't've been that. It must've been sick. The tar probably didn't have anything to do with any of it."

But she cried, "Yes!" and repeated, "Yes, yes," as she covered her face with her hands.

"It's just a bird," he said.

She looked up again, her dark eyes glazed, her face red. "All last evening, all this morning—we were—you don't know—we were so—*intimate!*"

"I know, of course. Look, I'll get a shovel," and he hurried down the steps as if he wanted to escape her show of grief. When he came back from the basement a few minutes later, he had not only a shovel but a rake, a pickax, a hatchet, a large hedge shears, and a hoe, all jumbled together in his arms, their prongs and tines and handles a confusion of metal and wood. She had wiped her eyes on the edge of her skirt again, and the excess color had drained from her face. She still knelt on the ground beside the box with the dead bird, but the violence of her grief had passed, and with its passing, she felt composed as she had not felt all that morning.

"What are you going to do with all those?" she asked.

"If we're going to stay here anyway, we ought to clean up this place a little, don't you think?"

"Oh."

He put down all his tools except the spade, picked up the box, and walked to the back of the garden. She stood up and then called to him, "But why bother, if it's only for a few months, as you say?"

He did not answer, but another voice did, Brenda White's, from behind the hedge. "Is my boy back?" the raucous voice called, and then was followed by the plump figure pushing through the privet.

"How'd he do?" she asked quietly of Helen.

"He failed."

Brenda made a dismal face. "So now?"

"So we stay another semester. I don't know how."

"Poor boy," she said, and walked back to where he was bending over his spade. For a moment Helen watched them—the plump, grotesquely dressed, motherly woman, with no children and no demands for herself; and the man, her own husband, bent to his task, the muscles moving easily under the smooth brown skin of his back as he dug. They seemed to be a pair, doting mother and son, and then, as Helen looked again across the water, to the city, and thought, To vanish now, simply to disappear, vanish! she added, in her thought, They *are* a pair. She stood on the edge of the little terrace, staring out ahead of herself as whole minutes passed, her face lifted and lighted.

"What's the matter?" Bill asked beside her.

"Matter?"

"You look—"

"Yes?"

"What are you going to do?"

"Do?"

"You're going to do something! What are you planning to do?"

She forced her eyes away from the distant smudge of smoke that still hung over the water where the boat had been and let them rest on his near presence, and in an instant she saw that, looking at her now, as he was, everything was going out of him; his face was extinguished. And she saw Brenda White, remote as a background figure in a picture, stooping at the back of the garden, patting that new grave with the flat of the shovel.

"Do?" she asked again, in faint surprise. "Do? Why—nothing." And she was shaken for a moment by a kind of pity for him.

"Ah," he sighed almost tonelessly, "but you are. What?"

She felt a flash of triumph and turned away from him again. Once more she looked at the blur of smoke on the bright-blue water, and then over it, to the towering city. In the evening, the mists would have returned to wrap that brightness once more in their soft blur. Tonight. And tonight she would be free in those fog-bound streets, deep in the cool, misty channels of the city, alone! Something in her positively sang.

And then there, where they were, across the bay from the white city, the sun burned through the last wisps of morning mist and suddenly set fire to the silly garden. Everything burned—every blade of grass was a flame, every wretched, neglected, paltry zinnia a flame, the rotten roses bursts of flame, a consummation, and as she felt herself swept up into this fire, free, transfigured, free of him, her exultation was so great that she turned and seized him by the naked shoulders, and then plunged into his astonished embrace.

GROTESQUE

*O*ne Sunday after our noon dinner, when I was about thirteen and Bill, my brother, fourteen or just fifteen, our father asked us to come down to his office at the canning factory with him. We were both dressed in the blue serge suits that we wore to church, and Father was dressed in his comparably austere garb. A stiff atmosphere of a queer "occasion" pervaded that short drive from our house to his office, and it was intensified as he ushered us in and asked us to sit down as he sat down behind his desk. Then came a remarkable speech. I wish that I had a recording of it, for the exact vocabulary. It was a horrid, embarrassing plea for approval, perhaps for love.

He began by saying that he knew that we thought that he treated our mother badly, but what we didn't know was how badly she had treated him. When he came to Sauk City, he listened to her sing in the church choir and he fell in love with her, this Jesus-praising virgin, and asked her to marry him. Just before they were to be married, some of his good Masonic "friends" took him aside and told him that she was reputed to be an easy lay (my word), that it was known that she had been had by at least one of the local gentry, who then married her best friend (I had often wondered why my father went out of his way to avoid speaking to this extremely genial man), and by a salesman or two who came to her mother's store. These included, even, a Jew! (And there was one man from Milwaukee—with whom, I think, my mother had been in love—who turned up later at a homecoming affair, and because she acknowledged his greeting in a perfectly casual if cordial way, a dreadful ruckus took place afterward and went on long into the night.) Bill and I listened to it all silently, even to that final bit about the Jew, when Father said that he brought it all up to our mother and asked her if it was true. He said that he told her that if it was, he would not marry her. She said that if he didn't, she would kill herself. So he did. Results known.

I'm not certain how Bill responded to all that since we never talked about it. (If he were alive, I'd ask him now; it's another of those questions I neglected to ask.) I do know that after that weird session, my mother had more of my love—and pity, alas—than she had had before, and that for the first time I judged my father not as the cruel but as the pathetic creature that, for the rest of his life, I thought that I knew him to be.

My judgment may well have been unfair. Looking back, I think that I never saw him for the simple man, not to say, probably, the simpleminded man that he was, brought up in, among other silly dogmas, that rigorous doctrine of "purity" before the holy sacrament of marriage. I am certain that he had kept himself "pure."

He was a "health" freak, for one thing. Over all the years that I recall, he subscribed to Bernarr Macfadden's *Physical Culture*, and over his desk he had a whole shelf of books about the human anatomy and how to keep it in condition. He was always exercising all over the place, doing pushups, chin-ups, etc., and working out with some primitive version of an isometric bar. He was always urging Bill and me to get down on the floor with him and do sit-ups or something. I was bored, and perhaps this explains why Bill became a very good athlete and I became one of the great examples of the non-athlete.

In at least one episode, Father's naïveté led to a situation that now seems grotesquely funny. He saw an ad in one of his periodicals that offered a pair of "championship" Belgian hares for $75, and the promise to buy back all of their offspring. Father thought that this would be a good enterprise for his boys and ordered a pair of the hares and built a most impressive rabbit hutch, two levels, with eight separate and ample cages with runways up to the second level. This considerable structure was installed in one corner of our vegetable garden, and the pair of rabbits arrived—handsome, delightful animals. But the procreation that began almost immediately was unbelievable. The larger rabbits, of which very soon there seemed to be six, eight, twelve, stomped around heedlessly, treading to death any number of the newly born creatures that were hopping about in the hope of survival. My brother and I struggled desperately to keep this slaughter under control, but then came winter, and now it was the weather that killed the little, endlessly spawned beasts, so charming. In the meantime, my father was writing almost nightly to the Belgian hare company, telling them about the number of splendid offspring that he was prepared to sell back to them. Of course, he never had a reply. Finally he understood that he had been duped and he persuaded the one local attorney to write the company, threatening suit for "using the mail to defraud." His $75 investment was presently returned, but there we were, with that great horde of rabbits. One day in good weather Father arrived in a factory truck, backed it up to the rabbit hutch, and we put all the rabbits —at least one hundred—into it. We then drove into the country, and at some wooded point Father pulled off the road, got out, opened the tailgate of the truck, and shoved all those hopping animals off into the ditch near the woods. The crops of the neighboring farmers must have been devastated for years. We drove back to Sauk City, and my grim father immediately began to dismantle his great architectural feat, the rabbit hutch. We all dug around later and planted tomatoes. It was probably very rich soil.

Now, remembering that folly, I do forgive him, if I had not years ago.

DON'T

TAKE ME

FOR GRANTED

Some wild-spice odor of wet bark or burned leaves or
earth, roots in the rot, both sweet and acrid—the wild
October night was full with some such odor, blowing in
gusts on the wind that raved through the black world. It
was a wind heavy and warm with moisture, but violent, too;
the limbs of trees groaned in it, ash cans banged, unhooked
shed doors rattled and slammed. And somewhere a dog
howled with abandoned melancholy.

Gilbert Miles, with three fire logs in his arms, leaned
against the side of the garage behind his house and laughed
weakly. The wind made him feel a queer inner release, a
sickening kind of happiness, and he threw back his head
and yelled into the crazy wind. He could feel the wind rip
the sounds away from him, right out of his mouth! And
some other sound that came to him now as a soft wail in
the wind was really his wife, Marian, her head thrust out
through a crack of the study doors, calling shrilly and quite
futilely. "Gilbert! Gilbert! For heaven's sake, where are
you?"

" 'Blow, winds, and crack your cheeks! Rage! Blow!' " Gilbert was, at the same time, yelling into the wind, with the sudden pleasure a boy takes in an unpremeditated shout. Then he laughed again, muttered, "Second childhood," and, lowering his head, bucked the wind as he made his way round the corner of the house. He found Marian at the French doors of the study, peering out into the darkness of the garden. She backed away as he entered. "For heaven's sake, Gilbert, where were you? You've been gone twenty minutes."

"Just out there," he said, tossing his head back as he crossed the small, book-lined room to kneel before the fireplace. He had left the doors open behind him, and the wind came leaping in. On the desk loose papers rattled and scattered before Marian could scamper to shut the doors. "You can yell and hardly hear yourself," he said as he put the logs on the embers.

Nor did she hear him then, in her eagerness to close the glass doors, fasten the latch, and pull the drapes. She went to his desk and picked up the typewritten sheets that had blown to the floor, and she said, "I would have cared much less if it had been anyone but Maggie Matthewson."

Gilbert stood up and gave her an inquiring look. "Oh," he said then, remembering, "we're still on that." He brushed flakes of wood and bark from his blue blazer, poked once at the logs as they began to shoot up flame, and returned to the leather chair where he had been sitting before. He seized one of the books he had piled beside his chair and with undue eagerness leafed through the pages. When he had come to the page he wanted, he relaxed and read with apparent interest.

"Maggie Matthewson—" his wife had just begun when he threw back his head and laughed.

"What's funny?" Marian asked. She was seated now in a low chair by the fire, knitting an Argyle sock for him, pink and gray and baby blue.

" 'During the brief residue of his life, he abandoned himself to literature and dissipation,' " Gilbert quoted from the page before him, and once more exploded in a laugh.

"What's that?"

"That's one Thomas Humphry Ward, on a scurrilous, rather lewd poet named Charles Churchill."

"Did he?"

"What?"

"Abandon himself to dissipation?"

"It's the combination that's funny," Gilbert said.

"Maggie Matthewson—"

"It gives me an idea," Gilbert interrupted her. He glanced at the shallow pile of typescript on his desk, neatly stacked now and safe under a round glass paperweight placed there by his wife. This was as much as he had written on his big, projected book, the history of taste in the eighteenth century, that great work that was to put him at the head of his field and at the top of his profession. The wind, rattling at the panes behind the drapes, drew his glance away.

Marian's needles bristled and flew in her fingers. "An idea?"

"I should include a lot of additional, extended notes—notes on the later history of certain special phenomena in public approval. Churchill, now. In his lifetime—"

The baying of the dog came faintly into the room like a distant, suffering cry.

"Maggie Matthewson. You know the sort of faculty wife she is. The know-everything type, the type who tells you what's going on in the Administration Building before the president has dreamed it up. I don't know where she gets her information. Candidly, we've disliked each other ever since that argument over where the College Teas should take place. You remember, Gilbert. She won out, and whenever we meet, she lets me feel her gloating still. Ugh!" Marian shuddered and with her wide eyes appealed to Gilbert for sympathy.

But Gilbert was staring into space, apparently oblivious of her, listening to the creak and groan of the trees in the garden. When, presently, he spoke, he said, "They said he was another Dryden. Yet not many years later, for Byron, at his grave, he was 'the comet of a season.' "

Marian's dark eyes narrowed with impatience, and as she spoke more sharply, her needles clicked with more rigid emphasis, as if she were scanning a poem in a schoolroom—*click* click *click* click *click* click-a-*click*. "She made a point of crossing the street to speak to me this afternoon. Went out of her way. Called and waved and came at a run. Only to say, 'My dear, I hear that Gilbert has *signed!*' Now, of course, everyone will know."

"I've made no attempt to hide the fact."

"She said, 'I'm astonished! I couldn't believe it. Gilbert, of all men! Why, he used to give those big, successful, money-raising parties for Adlai!' I pointed out that both of us were responsible for those parties, though, of course, it was your name that was on the letterheads. 'Well,' said she, 'you don't mean that Gilbert *isn't* a liberal, and *isn't* concerned with the real threat to his intellectual freedom that this oath, my dear, *is*, unquestionably *is!*' As though I, of course, know nothing of its implications. Oh, damn her!"

" 'The Glory and the Nothing of a Name,' said Byron," Gilbert said with warm good humor, and smiled at her benignly.

"I explained that the oath was mailed to you while you were away in the summer, and that the covering material made it sound—as everyone knows it did—as though the faculty approved. Of course, that's no reason. And you *wouldn't* have signed it, Gilbert, if I'd been with you there at the Houghton Library instead of here."

"Wouldn't I have?" he asked blandly.

"She said, 'Ah, but even though it's notarized, he can call it back. He can write the president, explain his misunderstanding, and ask that it be rescinded.' That's what Howard Henderson has done, she said. Gilbert, that's what you must do."

He listened to the repetitious thump-thump-thump of wood against wood outside somewhere. "That old cellar door, I think," he said, and started to get up.

"Don't go!" she said quickly. "Listen, Gilbert, will you? Have it rescinded, I mean. You just can't detach yourself from the right side of an issue like this. After all, think of all the organizations we've belonged to—A.C.L.U., for *years!* Why, we were even registered I.P.P. voters, until they proved so impossible. All the telegrams to congressmen . . ."

"Pussy, like the folk-dancing classes; that was always you, not me."

"But you do object to special oaths, and that sort of coercion!"

"Oh, sure, I do. It's damned nonsense. But I'm not a Communist, I never have been, and if it makes the president and the trustees happy to have me say so in front of a notary, I don't *care!*"

"Ah, but even Maggie Matthewson sees the catch there. *Now* it's Communism. The next time it will be something else. They're really telling you how to *think!* All of a sudden you won't be allowed to be an atheist! Gilbert, I shouldn't have to tell you these things."

"Don't," he said. Had the wind died down? He could, he thought, no longer hear the thumping door.

"The principle—don't you *believe* in acting on principle?"

In her eagerness, she had stood up, a slight, animated woman, tense, now, with conviction. Her knitting had dropped to the floor. Gilbert got up and retrieved it for her. Then he turned his back and stood over his desk. His hand touched the manuscript. He moved the paperweight and started to pick up the sheets. Instead, he only flipped the stacked edge with his thumb, and he swung around suddenly with all the color gone from his rather long, narrow face, his jaw hanging.

"What's the matter?" she cried.

"The way things suddenly come to you," he said quietly.

"What are you talking about?"

"I'm forty-four, and at sixty-five I'll be one of those old men, full of winter and antiquarian information, and I'll be eager to retire, I'll say, so that, at last, I can finish the famous life work."

She came to him quickly and put her hand on his arm. To look up at his face now, she had to let her head drop back. "What you've said is *just* to my point. You're forty-four. I'm nearly forty. At our age—Gilbert, what *except* principle do we have to live for?"

He smiled wanly. "But I have no principles of the kind you're talking about any more." He said it as gently as if he were telling her he loved her.

She turned away and sat down angrily. "Then," she said, "there's nothing, just nothing at all!"

His face lightened. "There's this," he said with sudden recollection. "Came today." He put his hand inside his jacket and drew out a letter, a gray tissue envelope, with incisive black strokes—his name and campus address—written across it. He handed it to her.

She read. "Dear Professor Miles: I will be in the city this weekend, and I have taken a suite at the Gotham Hotel. On Saturday I am giving a cocktail party in your honor. I have asked twenty-seven girls, all me, and please plan to stay for breakfast. Yours, S.H."

Marian looked up in bewilderment. "What is this? Who is S.H.?"

"S.H. stands for Susan Hardy. That bright girl in my seminar."

"Is she asking *you*— Is she asking you to— Is she *actually* asking—"

"Yes."

"Why, the child's mad!"

He smiled, and he heard the wind come up again outside and, again, the thump-thump-thump of the loosened door. "She's not a child. She's twenty-seven. That's what she means, I suppose, about the twenty-seven girls, all her. Rather a whimsical type, you know. She's been a buyer for a department store. Men's accessories no less. Smart, quite pretty, only a little plump, perhaps." And with that he pulled back the drapes and once more opened the French doors onto the garden.

"Gilbert, where are you going now?"

"To fasten that door," he said, and took a deep breath of the wild night smell.

Then a sharp gust of wind blew in, and this time, with a great shuffling in the air, like a flock of gulls trapped in the room, the entire manuscript lifted and scattered through the windy space.

"Oh, Gilbert," Marian cried in dismay, "you're so careless! Close the doors!" She fell to her knees and began to reassemble the sheets. "Of course, you'll have to report that girl to the deans, won't you? Whatever her age, she's clearly mad! *Please* close the doors!"

Slowly he turned around. "Don't bother with those papers," he intoned in a funeral voice, "and don't take so much for granted, Pussy dear." She stared up at him. "So, I think, possibly, am I."

He stood in the open door, facing the room now, looking down at her where she was disadvantaged on her knees. The wind blew at the curtains and it blew at him. It shook the deep folds of faded maroon rep, and it moved the soft flannel folds of his blazer.

"Mad, you mean?" she asked, as she scrambled up, and looking at him with a start, she saw that, indeed, in a sense, he was. She shivered with sudden fright, and fifteen years of past and habit shook in her like leaves. The October wind roared, a shutter banged, the dog bayed long and mournfully, its wail mounting to a thin and vibrant scream, and a sudden reversal of air currents filled the room with a belch of smoke. Marian was experiencing the curious sensation of feeling as small as she was, and as helpless as she was small. Everything was abruptly strange, and how implausible she sounded, even to herself, as, changing her tack, she decided to say with trembling brightness, "Pussy! Remember, dear, when you first called me that? It was . . . Shut the doors now and . . . !" But her words trailed off and jolted into a sob as she watched invisible fingers play through the long, thinning strands of his hair, and saw the autumn blackness yawning behind him, a cave of winds.

" U N C L E "

Dr. Marcus Bossard was not really my uncle, but that was what I had been brought up to call him, Uncle Marcus. He had married my mother's aunt, Bertha, a younger sister of Selina Jaeger, my grandmother, *geborene* Homberger. Uncle Marcus, after whom I was named (again, shadowy hopes of a fortune that never materialized!), lived in Spring Green. He was a bluff, hearty man, and also a man of considerable cultivation. He loved music and he played the piano in a bold, rather splashy, and to me very exciting fashion, very different from my mother's light tinkle-tinkle-tinkle touch. He introduced me to Beethoven's sonatas. He went often to Milwaukee and Chicago to hear operas and concerts, and he would try to convey to me his sense of the wonders of opera. He said that some time he would take me along so that I could experience them directly. (This never happened; the first operas I heard were in Boston in 1930, with, among others whom I don't now remember, Mary Garden, singing *Louise* and *Pelléas et Mélisande*. I can hear her now as, fleeing through blue mists, she cries, "*Je ne suis pas heureuse ici.*") He talked to me about the beauties of the oboe and the bassoon, instruments of which I had never heard but which seemed to have a special fascination for him. And he must have thought that I had some musical talent, or, at least, that my interest in his accounts and his piano performances could be doctored into a talent. At any rate, when I was graduated from high school in 1925, he gave me an oboe.

Alas, the fact is that I have no musical talent. Years of piano lessons came to nothing. Several years of violin lessons came to nothing. Even laborious efforts with a mandolin came to nothing. (My ambition was to serenade a girl, Helen Steadman, with whom I was for a long time infatuated, in a rowboat; no one in that town had a canoe.) And now there was this oboe. It came with a self-instruction manual and a group of exercises and tunes. During that summer I made every effort to master that oboe for a very special reason. That September I was to enroll at the University of Wisconsin. If one was admitted to the university orchestra, one was exempt from the alternative physical education or military training requirements. These possibilities seemed equally loathsome to me and I asked for an audition for the orchestra. The director said that my oboe was a poor one but that the university could let me have a better one, and since there was no other oboist in sight, I was admitted. In one orchestral work—Tchaikovsky, I think —I even had a short solo, great moment. But the orchestra doubled as the marching band, and the band marched at football games and other athletic events, and oboists, with that sharp double reed, do not march. For that reason, I was made one of the cymbal clashers whenever we marched. I believe that I mastered the cymbals.

The Homberger family consisted of Robert (my middle name, since he was an affluent local banker; my *Tauf-Schein*

—baptismal certificate—shows him to have been one of the witnesses at that occasion); Selina, my grandmother; Rose, who was married to someone named Hoppe and lived in Wausau, the mother of Wanda, a church organist and an educated woman; and Bertha Bossard.

Aunt Bertha (for whom my sister was named), whom I could not have known beyond my sixth or seventh year, had a kind of glamour. Rather plump, full-breasted, red-cheeked, blond hair piled high, exploding with laughter and generally giving out the sense of her pleasure in living, she went occasionally to Germany. The last time, probably 1914, she became ill on the return passage and died on shipboard. Her body was sent back to Spring Green, and our family drove there from Sauk City for the funeral. I remember only the open coffin in front of the great square piano: it was the first corpse I had seen. She owned rather splendid German jewelry which Uncle Marcus gave to my mother. He was theatrical in his grief. She was buried in the Sauk City cemetery and he commissioned an ostentatious monument for her grave, a "Rock of Ages" figure clinging to a cross, seven or eight feet tall, towering over every other grave marker in that cemetery. Later, when he remarried, my parents said that it embarrassed him, and when he died, he was not buried beside her, although his place was laid out there in that lot and space left vacant on the base of the monument for his name and dates. But long before that he employed a housekeeper named Nelly, a jolly young woman, to run his establishment and keep his office in order, one half of the front of his house. It was she who attended to me in the three or four weeks of each summer that, for reasons unknown to me, I spent there.

Why, as a boy of eight and nine and ten, I was sent to Spring Green in the summers is not, as I say, quite clear to me. Perhaps because he was childless, Uncle Marcus liked to have a youngster around. More likely, it was simply to get at least one child out from underfoot at home, especially now that there was a third child, my sister, in that most hectic part of the year (the canning season, and my father in his perpetual rages).

But it was such a thing! At that time a two-car train came into Sauk City on our spur line twice a day, not chiefly to accommodate passengers, but to take out and bring in mail and small freight. I would be put on the morning train with a packed telescope suitcase. For a few years the suitcase was made of wicker, but that must have collapsed because later it was of gray canvas. The train would chug down to Mazomanie, nine miles away, where I had to change trains and, in due time, get onto another which chugged to and through Arena and came presently to Spring Green—a total distance of perhaps twenty miles, but a good half day or more from the time I left Sauk City. There, at the Spring Green station (or depot, as we called it), I was met by Nelly and Uncle Marcus.

I enjoyed their cuisine, so different from ours, more various, more delicate. It was at their table that I first tasted sage cheese, that hard, stone-like orb from which one scrapes those deliciously spicy shavings to spread on buttered bread. But generally my recollections of those summers are vague. How did I spend most of my time? Did I have any playmates? Who knows? But two sharp images remain with me.

One morning I came down to the kitchen and Nelly was looking out of a window, across the back garden to a stable that backed up to it from a parallel street. A man's limp body, gently moving, was hanging from a rafter by a noose. "Don't look!" she said, as I looked.

My uncle was Frank Lloyd Wright's physician when Wright was in residence at Taliesin, and one day when he was scheduled to make a call there he took me out with him. I had a sense of the mystery and the tragedy if not of the greatness that adhered to that place. Only a few years before, in 1914, Wright's black cook, Julian Carlston, had suddenly gone mad and murdered six people with an ax and seriously wounded four more, then burned the cottage in which these people, most of them children but including their mother, Wright's mistress, were living. The shock of this horrendous act swept across Wisconsin and the entire Middle West, and in the surrounding countryside it reached the ears even of a six-year-old, as I then was. Wright as a consequence had taken on something like legendary proportions in my imagination. He did not disappoint me now. I could not have been more impressed than when, just as we got out of our car, Wright came charging over a hill on a white horse, pulling up abruptly beside us, sliding out of his saddle, and greeting my uncle. Horses were familiar enough, but not riding horses, certainly not such a shining white horse as this, nor such a man, white-haired already, wearing a white shirt with open Byronic collar and white jodhpurs, and appearing, as in a story or a film, so dramatically.

This was my first meeting with a great man. Years later, 1946, when I met him for the only other time at a reception for him in San Francisco, we chatted about Uncle Marcus Bossard, then quite recently dead.

A LAMP

An Italian lamp can be an object of extraordinary ugliness. This is an order of ugliness that is not to be found in nature but must result from deliberate, perversely original human invention and contrivance, as if each time he put himself to the task, the designer had said to himself, "Now get with it, signor, and see if you can come up with a *real* horror!"

Franklin Green had had such thoughts before. He had them again as he contemplated with a certain intensity of gaze—almost a glare—such a lamp. It stood on the edge of the *salone* of a Roman apartment where, on one side of the unlighted hearth, he, holding an empty cocktail glass, sat in a large chair covered with yellow satin and framed in carved, gilded wood. With what was almost a physical tug, he pulled his eyes away from the lamp to his glass and then to the table in front of his chair where he busied himself with ice, vodka, vermouth, and a saucer of lemon peel.

Flora, his wife, who sat on the other side of the hearth

in an identical chair, thought in a vein similar to his as she, too, stared at the lamp. Such an object, she was thinking, is no accident. Behind it might lie a lifetime of mistaken effort, and the motive of that effort might be malice or spleen or even some kind of abstract vengeance. There was something absolutely cruel about it. Engrossed, she did not look down at once at the replenished cocktail glass her husband put before her. He had continued across the room to stand at one of the open pairs of French doors that gave onto a generous terrace and to stare out over tiled Roman roofs. In the deepening summer twilight, swifts incessantly wheeled and cried.

Franklin Green was a tall man, but the lamp behind him stood taller than he—nearly seven feet. It was made of painted wrought iron and pretended to be a gigantic stalk of lilies. It was the pretense of imitating nature that made it so alarmingly unnatural. The spindly stem, not much more than a half inch in thickness, was pea green, and at six regular intervals sprouted sets of two narrow, dangerously pointed leaves. Then, about five feet from the floor, the thing burst into a horror of iron blossoms. There were five five-petaled, full-blown lilies, each about eight inches across, painted white, their veined petals arching back, and in the center of each, three metal prongs with a yellow knob at the end of each—pistils or stamens, which? There was also one absurd, aspiring bud, just opening. Above all this was the single twenty-five-watt bulb, only partially concealed by a pleated silk shade, disproportionately small and narrow, perched there like some halfhearted, grudging afterthought.

The first time one of the Greens had turned on the lamp, it had spluttered and blown out the main fuse in the apartment. Since then, the cord with its disconnected plug was looped over the set of leaves nearest the spindly-legged tripod that formed the base.

The lamp was all the more remarkable in that there was nothing else in this apartment, which was otherwise quite smartly furnished, that seemed to be related to it. It existed in grotesque isolation. The other lamps, smaller objects on tables and chests, were not beautiful, but they were unobtrusive and even gave a rather decent light when one remembered that they were, after all, Italian. There were many other things on which the eye could rest with comfort: three fine Piranesi prints hung in a row; decent vases; a gilt screen with tapestry panels; the large, arched, truly elegant mirror over the fireplace. But it was the lamp that always commanded the Greens' attention. Franklin Green had turned and, glass in hand, was staring at it again.

"Let's move it out," Flora had said early in their stay, after it had proved at once to be as useless as it was horrid. For a day or two, indeed, they had it in their bedroom, since there seemed to be no other place, no storage closet or cupboard where it could be put out of sight, and they could hardly add it to the clutter of the maid's tiny room off the kitchen. But in their bedroom it made Flora positively uneasy, and after those two days, Franklin moved it again into its corner of the living room. And so, whenever they were in that room, they found themselves staring at it, thinking similar thoughts about it, laughing at it, jeering at it as *la lampada* and *il lampadone*—the great big lamp—but also beginning faintly and unaccountably to brood.

The apartment was in the Via Giulia and the Greens had signed a six-month lease for it, half of a strange year in their lives. They had been in Europe a number of times before, together and separately, but never for such an extended stay and never so inseparably.

Franklin Green was a successful attorney in his middle fifties, Flora was five years younger. They had been married for over twenty-five years and their two daughters were married in turn, each now beginning her own family, one in Connecticut, the other in California. When the younger girl married almost immediately after the older one, the Greens felt themselves free but, in a rather uncomfortable way, unnecessary. More than that, Franklin had been suffering from a depletion of energy that he had never experienced before. For three years he had worked hard on a complicated corporation tax case that had him in Washington nearly as much as he was in New York, and his doctor had suggested that a long vacation was in order. With the successful conclusion of the case at last, his partners had agreed to a year's leave when the Greens had decided that now, before they were even one year older, was the time really to *do* Europe. After all, why not?

Their marriage had been uneventful and unusually companionable. Most of their friends had been divorced at least once and remarried, often in a glitter of scandal, but the idea of separation had never entered the mind of either Franklin or Flora Green, not even as an impossibility. There was something inevitable about their union, and there had been from the start.

Flora had been a friend and classmate of Franklin's younger sister at Vassar. He met her one summer when she came for a week as a guest in his parents' house at Quogue. She was a tall, athletic girl, good at tennis and golf, in the surf and on a horse, with fine long legs and a handsome face—high cheekbones, amused brown eyes, loosely combed chestnut hair. Their interests, like their height, suited them to one another and they found themselves together all that week. Not long out of law school and a junior member of his Wall Street firm, Franklin saw a good deal of her in the following autumn and winter. In the spring, her last at Poughkeepsie, she began to spend her weekends with him in his bachelor apartment on East End Avenue. On Sunday noons she would make quite a thing of "brunch," scrambling eggs for him in a special way and serving them with a green salad, and then they'd have a long, leisurely afternoon in a museum or at the movies. They had gay and easy times together and she enjoyed fussing over him—organizing his possessions, cataloguing his records, straightening out his books, replacing missing buttons. Marriage was hardly discussed; it was simply assumed, as if decreed, and it took place promptly after her graduation in June.

They had leased a slightly larger apartment in his old building and it was as if hardly anything had been changed. Then, all during the war years, he occupied a Navy desk in Washington, and there the children were born. Then New York again, a senior partnership, the new and much larger apartment on Fifth Avenue between Eighty-eighth and Eighty-ninth Streets, the career, the bringing up of the little girls, then the big girls, the death of parents, the house at Quogue theirs, the career, the girls young women, married, gone. Now it all seemed remote, even rather characterless, and sometimes, here in the Roman apartment with the grotesque, inescapable lamp, Flora could hardly remember what that other apartment in New York, all sheeted and shaded in their absence, was like. And her past, all those years, where was it, *what* was it, she would vaguely wonder as she stared at the lamp.

Well, they had been serene years, and she and Franklin were friends, and the idea of a year together in Europe seemed splendid. After all, why not? Simply lock up the place and go, seize their freedom now that they had it! With a whole year, it would not be the usual hectic scrambling of American tourists abroad. They would take their time, do only what they wanted to do; it would be a long vacation, a ball.

Half the year, they had decided, was to be spent in Italy, and most of that in a single city—Rome, it had developed, after they discovered what a clutter Florence had become. In the first half of the year, they would go briefly to other places, and perhaps that had been their error. They became the victims of some self-imposed acceleration they could not hold back, almost as if at first they were made restless and uneasy by being alone together and had to keep moving to occupy themselves. Those first six months had deteriorated into just the kind of packing-unpacking, hotel-heaped-upon-hotel jumble that they had meant to avoid. In five months they had been in eight countries—fifty cities, sixty, a hundred? they could hardly say—and in the sixth month, as if now they were wound up by the first five and could not come to a halt, in nearly all the northern cities of Italy, with a few resort towns thrown in for good measure— Genoa, Portofino, Cernobbio, Milan, Garda, Vicenza, Venice, Padua, Verona, Mantua, Ferrara, Ravenna, Bologna, Pisa, Florence—but Florence even more briefly than most of the others. Fifteen years before, when the ruins of the war still lay tumbled along the Arno, they had spent nearly a month there and loved it, and so they had thought of settling there now for their half year. But the contrast with the Florence of their more youthful visit was too painful. You couldn't *walk* in Florence any more! Rome, noisy and crowded and impersonal as it was, was much better; they were living at last in a leisurely, pleasant way, adjusted to one another as even they had never been, sitting here now, for example, having their quiet cocktails, the birds crying outside as they careened through the twilight, and inside, the room all softened and charming . . . except for the *lampada!*

But then, what of all that had come before Italy, or, for that matter, before Rome? It was, they frequently confessed to one another, a mad confusion, as if they were drowning in a kaleidoscope of their own shattered impressions. Castles, cathedrals, gardens, galleries, pictures, stairways, statues, spires, towers, domes, ruins—all pieces, shifting, circling, jiggling in and out of the mind, jumbled together.

Their last excursion in Germany, just before flying into Italy, had been to Schloss Nymphenburg on the edge of Munich. They had seen the film *Last Year at Marienbad* and, like everyone they knew, had been interested, irritated, and confused by it; they wanted to see the place where it had been filmed. Now, as Franklin gave Flora her third cocktail, a little tipsy in a gently melancholy way, she said, "You know, it's curious. Out of the entire jumble, what remains most clearly with me is Nymphenburg—a kind of elegant jumble itself."

"Yes. It does for me, too." He was looking serious, his heavy, graying eyebrows pulled together as if he were working out some vexing problem. "The hunting lodge especially. Those tidy little cubicles for dogs in the first room. Imagine keeping dogs inside a place like that! With that silver ballroom. Or concert room, was it? It's clear as anything. Then finally the kitchen."

"Just before you enter the ballroom, or concert room—I can't remember the function either, but it's the great, beautiful, round room, all mirrors and silver—just before you enter, there's that other room, all yellow gold and silver, with a kind of bed built into a tall niche in the wall, remember?"

"Yes. A place for the princess, returned from the hunt, to rest. The only place, apparently. It's hard to imagine the daily life, isn't it?"

"Remember how we searched for the statue that was so prominent in the movie—of the man and woman? And which was leading which? And not finding it?"

"Something added, we decided. A necessary prop. It had to be added for the sake of the story."

"Story?"

He laughed, and so did she, but then her still rather

noble face became sober at once as she pushed her fingers through her abundant hair, held back by a black velvet band, and went on to say, "I feel every now and then that I'm *in* that film."

"I think I know what you mean."

"It's as if I'm that camera, registering all that splendor, but only registering it. Stairs, walls, corridors, plaster, gardens . . . Remember how the voice intoned those catalogues? That's me."

"I know what you mean," he said. Suddenly he found himself looking at her. Something in her distracted tone had drawn his eyes to her, and he was *looking* at her. This was a shock because with it he knew that he had not really looked at her for years. He had always seen her, of course, but in a way he had not been seeing *her*. Her eyes were settled on the lamp, and he wondered if she saw it, they looked so vacant, so empty of everything except a vague, remote bewilderment. In her neck were lines that he had never noticed, a little tuck of skin under her chin, lines of laughter beside her mouth, some white in the reddish-brown hair, and in her earlobes, pearl clips that were new to him. But she may have had them for a decade! He had become like the camera, too, apparently—registering, but merely registering, and not Europe alone. In his mild shock, this most familiar figure in his life seemed suddenly strange to him, a stranger.

She started a little and so did he. Then both, as with an agreed resolve, swallowed the rest of the cocktails, and as they put down their glasses, they said in unison, "Shouldn't we go?" They laughed again.

"My God!" exclaimed Franklin, and "Yes!" Flora answered, with another laugh, and they glanced at their watches, "Past eight-thirty," they agreed as they started from the room, but not without a last look at the lamp, as if they needed its consent to go out for dinner.

When they reached the street, it was dark and the swifts were gone. But it was dark with a difference. Almost at once the Greens saw that the great street lamps, jutting out at regular intervals on scrolled iron arms fixed in palazzo walls, were not lit. Here and there a shop window leaked out a faint blur of light on the paving stones, but above, the heavy Renaissance buildings loomed black as the night itself, and the street had never seemed so narrow.

"Power failure?" Franklin speculated as they paused outside their enormous arched entry. Flora took his arm and they began a careful walk up the street on its uneven, treacherous stones. They were going to the restaurant, very near them, which they most often frequented—good food and service, quiet, discreet music, no wandering minstrels or flower vendors offering single roses for a hundred lire but hoping for five, or grown men selling silly balloons. In one month, the restaurant had become a kind of habit with them. It was restful, almost a retreat. Busy, jostling, daytime Rome disappeared there. They felt at home, comfortable. It was a habit now.

Abruptly they came to a halt. They were outside an antique shop that they had passed many times without particularly noticing, but tonight, with the street in darkness, the brilliance of its interior illumination through the single very large window stopped them. It was like a stage in a darkened theater, but a stage with its lights turned on at full blaze. Every item of furniture and decoration—a black armoire appliquéd with elaborate scrolls of mother-of-pearl, a commode with ormolu mounts, two long case clocks with intricate marquetry, a torchère in the window that held an ormolu clock in the shape of an urn, its pendulum swinging swiftly, and from the ceiling, a veritable crystal arbor of glittering lusters—each of these and other objects stood out sharp and clear, and each as if it had its own illumination. One item did: a Canova-like bust of a woman, set in a concave circular niche above a door at the back of the room, a niche with concealed lighting that gave the marble a cold white glitter, a special dead brilliance within the general blaze.

"Like a stage," Flora murmured. "And there seems to be a play going on, too."

There were two characters, apparently the proprietors. At the back of the room and to one side was a mahogany secretary not very different from two others in the shop except that it was used, with paper on its dropped front and papers in its pigeonholes. At the desk sat a very beautiful young woman with ink-black hair and a magnolia-white face, her right elbow on the edge of the desk, her pen in her hand in midair, as if she had just been interrupted in the act of writing, her head turned, lips parted, her black, heavily shadowed eyes looking up with intense concentration. She was looking at a young man who stood in a doorway beside the desk, leaning indolently against the frame. He was as casual as she was intent. He was elegantly dressed in a moderately sporting way, and his careful hair, his trim brown mustache and short beard, even the polished nails on his extended hand, suggested that he had just left his barber. Or the makeup man. In that brilliant interior, they both looked as though they were made up, the individual features highlighted, defined.

Whatever he was saying had galvanized her attention. He seemed to be speaking slowly, with the suggestion of a smile, his hand hardly moving. This was not one of those passionate, profuse verbal exchanges in which Italians seemed forever to be explaining something to someone else. On his part, it was like a meditation; on hers, an offering to receive. Now she put down the pen without taking her eyes from his face and stood up. The top of her head came to about his shoulders, so that, standing close to him, she had still to lift her head to look at him, and he to bend his. Now she was speaking, having seized his extended hand in both hers. His smile broadened; she began to smile. Then both, for a moment, were silent, and they simply stood there, completely engrossed, engaged.

That was it! it came to the Greens as they watched in the dark street. The drama was in the intense involvement, the absorption of one in the other, each so strikingly distinct in the bright glare, each so handsomely individual, and yet with a relatedness that presented itself to the Greens as a nearly physical thing in the air between the two, visible vibrations like heat waves.

"I feel that we're intruders," Flora whispered, and they began to walk again.

"Something extraordinary was going on there," said Franklin, who felt suddenly sad, as if he had lost something that he treasured.

"I feel sad," said Flora.

An hour and a half later, after a dinner of many courses and with nearly a liter of fine Frascati, as they waited for the man to bring Franklin's change, they were both yawning. That day they had made one of their usual planned excursions: to the National Gallery, then up to Borromini's church with one of the Four Fountains built into its corner, on to Bernini's circular church in the Via del Quirinale, and ending in the Piazza del Quirinale (where, they learned, they had seen what was perhaps the finest façade of one Ferdinando Fuga)—all very close together, but still tiring. Even a short Roman walk, with its almost inevitable little climb, was tiring, and they were weary. "Rome eats up heels," Flora's nice cobbler had said to her one day. *Roma consuma i tacchi!*

All the shops on the Via Giulia, including the cobbler's, were closed as they went down it, the shutters pulled and locked, but the street lights were on now. As the

Greens walked its length, their feet seemed to thrust their long, thin shadows ahead of them until they were so long and thin that they vanished in the stones, but then, rhythmically, they appeared immediately again beside them, thick and dark, only to grow attenuated once more. When they passed the antique shop, they did not mention the vivid scene that they had observed there earlier, but each of them thought about it. In their apartment, after a perfunctory look around, Franklin fixed the terrace shutters for the night and the Greens were ready for bed.

They had not been in their beds more than five minutes when they were both nearly asleep, but then Flora began drowsily to murmur.

"Our name is Green . . ." she murmured.

He started from his doze. "What?"

"Now I know why they called me Flora."

"I don't get you." He leaned up on his elbow, wide awake.

But more sleepily than ever, as if she were not talking to him at all, she said, "The lamp. Flora Green. It means something, the lamp . . ."

"You've lost me."

"Green and flowers. Flora Green . . ."

"Oh, come!" Softly.

"And Franklin Green . . ."

She was asleep, but he was now wide awake, and staring into the darkness over her head, he saw a vivid image of the *lampada,* as clear in its every detail as any of those antique objects in the shop, as if it were really there, and even when he closed his eyes hard, he was still scrutinizing it, as if indeed it were.

Some odd things had happened to the Greens. Flora, for example, often felt curiously adrift, as if the more crowded her mind and senses were with new impressions of old things, the more empty she became of herself, and not only of herself but of her past, which in itself came to seem nearly empty, and certainly very far away. It was as if the great ponderous past in which they were living was robbing her of her shorter, thinner past.

Franklin, for his part, was experiencing inertia, curious in a man who for so many years had kept himself busy in his profession and active in his physical life. When they first projected their year abroad, he was afraid that he would chafe when he found himself cut off from these habitual activities for so long a time. But not at all. Whether it had to do with his age—was that the time for men, the middle fifties?—or with his recent rundown state, or whether the two were related, he did not know, but the fact was that he was quite content to substitute for his old routines these new activities of galleries, monuments, museums, restaurants, ruins. When it was occasionally necessary for him to communicate with his office, in response to an inquiry from someone there, he rather impatiently dictated a nearly perfunctory reply to a public stenographer (he had found an able one in a Via Veneto hotel) and let it go at that. Without his files and his library, it was difficult to be really helpful; furthermore, he could not take these inquiries very seriously. His habitual life, somewhat like Flora's, seemed also to have slid away into the distance, paled out.

In this condition they were completely comfortable with one another and content to seek no further company. At first, in London and Paris, they had hunted up New York connections, but as they progressed on their journey, they did this less and less. Now they were almost always together and almost always alone. They had been in Rome for a month, and at least half a dozen acquaintances of theirs were there in residence, and they had letters to a dozen more, but they had done nothing about either possibility. "After all," Flora sighed on occasion, when a name was mentioned, "we didn't come to Europe to be with a lot of Americans." But they were not, of course, being with Europeans either.

If they were not making the acquaintance of many Romans, they were making a nearly systematic acquaintance of Rome itself. As soon as they had found and settled into their apartment, one of them had said to the other, "From here on, we've got to do things more deliberately, more self-consciously, or we're going to end up with nothing at all."

"Agreed!"

And Franklin said, "I think I'll get a notebook and start keeping a record."

"A diary?"

"No, just a record. Notes on what interests me. Just writing these things down may help me to remember them and keep them separate in my mind."

"Splendid."

He bought his notebook and almost every day found him making his faithful notations. He enjoyed this effort and he decided that it was helping him to see more and to see more closely than he had before. He knew a little about architecture, and most of his notes were about buildings—churches, palaces, temples—and the remains of buildings. What he put down was descriptive, matter-of-fact, and it contained little that he did not find in his guidebook. Often he echoed the guidebook, but he wrote only after he himself had observed the details to which it directed him, and the fact that it was his own writing was important. He studied closely a reconstruction of the Forum and the ground plans in his guidebook, and then, wandering endlessly back and forth in the Forum for an entire day, made his own plan of it on a double page of his notebook while Flora sat placidly watching him from various fallen stones.

Flora took to buying postcards of everything that she

particularly liked, chiefly paintings, and she began to write on the back of them. "I have no vocabulary for art," she said, "but if I can just put down my own impression, maybe I can keep these things separate, too, as you do the churches and so on."

"Good," said he.

"What I must remember is that every great work is an individual creation, a unique thing, like nothing else."

"Yes."

"It's true, isn't it, that every living work has its own special quality, its own character? And if it doesn't have it, it's dead, not art but an artifact?"

"I suppose so."

"And, Franklin—that's what's so awful about the *lampada* there. It's an extreme case. A dull imitation of something real, of something that is lovely in nature, and that's why it's so dead, so grotesquely artificial."

"Perhaps," he said uneasily.

"But to pinpoint the special quality in a given painting, I'd be helped by a real vocabulary. Some of the things I write sound just silly."

"I doubt it," he said.

"Schoolgirlish."

"Now don't get self-conscious in that way."

"And sometimes, even when I get a real charge from a picture or a statue, I have nothing to say, or I can't say what I feel. Like the enormous Pompey in the Spada."

"Just put down the approximate measurements, then, or some other simple physical facts," Franklin said. "Anything to help remember it clearly. Don't try to describe the expression."

"Pictures are easier," she said.

"Some are."

She looked through her growing stack of cards as he turned his attention to his notebook. Every now and then

she would draw one out of the pile and silently read what
she had written.

"Caravaggio. *Narcissus*. The young man absolutely
sick with yearning for himself. The painting of the sleeve—
the texture. The bright spot of blue in the deep shadow
above the pool. Codpiece?" She had since studied a large
reproduction, and now, flushing, she crossed out the last
word and wrote, "No. The other knee. One knee is bare.
This one clothed." And then she added, "I've learned that
this is probably not Caravaggio at all. C. didn't like blue."

Franklin glanced up at her. He was troubled. It was
the day after she had fallen asleep murmuring about their
names and the lamp—he glanced over her head to the
lamp, angrily—and he had said nothing about the matter.
Nor had she, even just now, when she had been talking
about the thing. He wondered if she knew.

She was reading her words on another card. "Borghese. *Leda*. Unknown painter. Probably after Leonardo.
The swan absolutely domesticated. A family man, the
pompous husband, and that naked girl's complete servant.
The twin boys in the grass. Helen's egg still unhatched,
behind them, as if forgotten. Other birds standing around.
A very comic picture. It gives joy and laughter."

When he closed his notebook she put her cards away.
"Do we pursue Zucchi today?"

"There's only one left. In a church called San Giovanni Decollato. *John the Beheaded*."

"Shall we?"

"Why not?"

This was one of their systematic projects—to hunt out
all the work of a given artist. They had seen every Caravaggio in Rome and he was now their favorite painter. A few
days before, they had found themselves amused in the
Borghese Gallery by two extravagant allegorical paintings by
someone they had never heard of, a presumably minor

Florentine named Zucchi, and now they were pursuing the Zucchis, of which there were not nearly so many as there were Caravaggios, and they did not expect this fantastic fellow to replace him in their affections. About Caravaggio they felt positively possessive, but only tolerant of this other one, entertaining as he was.

It was in the cab on the way to the Piazza Bocca della Verità, which was as close to the obscure street of San Giovanni Decollato as they could direct the driver, that Flora suddenly asked, "What was that dream again?"

"What dream?"

"You told me this morning. About the antique shop."

"What about it?"

"You said you had this dream in which you could hear what those people were saying."

"Flora, you're crazy. I said nothing of the kind. I didn't have a dream."

"But I thought . . ."

"It must have been your dream. What *did* they say?"

"I don't know . . . Did I dream it?"

"You must have. I didn't."

"I think you did. I think you've forgotten. I'm sure you told me about it just as we were waking up."

He laughed abruptly. "That'll be the day!"

"What?"

"When we start having each other's dreams."

The cab pulled to a stop beside a fountain. Paying and getting out, they dropped the matter.

"Let's have another look at the Truth Mouth since we're here," Franklin said, and they walked over to study the curious object through the grille that protected it. The flat round face with its staring eyes and open lips made Flora shudder. "I have the most awful feeling that it's going to start telling me something!"

"It does look as though it could talk. What would it say?"

"Yes, what?"

Silence, while they looked. He broke it with, "You were doing some strange talking last night."

"I? When?"

"When you were falling asleep. Or perhaps you were asleep. You don't remember?"

"No. What was I saying?"

"Something about a connection between your name— our names—and the *lampada*."

"What?"

"I don't know quite. 'Flora Green,' you were saying, and 'The lamp, it means something.' You don't remember?"

She looked puzzled. "Yes . . . yes . . . vaguely. I must have been on the very edge of sleep."

"Well?"

"I've thought it before, but not quite like that."

"Thought what?"

"The lamp wouldn't bother us so much if it didn't have some meaning."

"But what meaning? It's just a frightful lamp."

"Yes, it's that for sure."

Suddenly she turned from the wall with the head and looked directly and hard and freshly into his eyes. In dismay she said, "Franklin, you're tired!"

"Not particularly," he replied. "Let's go."

The curious thing that he had half jokingly suggested in the cab did in fact happen to them at some time during that night. When they were at breakfast next morning, Flora said, "Well, last night I did dream it."

"The antique shop," he said at once.

"Yes."

"Only we were the characters, not those others."

She looked at him in alarm. "Yes."

"Only we weren't talking, were we? We were sitting among all that furniture, all the glitter and the polish, the little gold clock with its pendulum swinging, the white bust smiling, everything there—we were sitting . . ."

"With our backs to each other," she finished for him.

"Yes," he said. "And . . . ?"

"Under the *lampada*."

They stared at one another and neither of them laughed. Either one of them might have made the next remark, since both were thinking it. It happened to be Flora who said, "We've been in too many countries." Each was aware that the observation was hardly adequate to the situation as they looked away from one another and waited for the next remark, which again might have been made by either of them: We should leave here now, adjust this lease, change our reservations, go back. Then each of them would hear the final word echo into a question: Back?

And neither would ask it aloud.

DECADENCE

*W*hen and how did I get involved with August Derleth? I was a year and a few months older than he, so that we were in different high-school classrooms. I was no brighter than he, I would think, but, with an older brother, probably more knowledgeable, whereas Aug had only a younger sister. Our friendship very likely began because, even as grade-school students, we both haunted the one-room public library on Saturday afternoons, when it was open. Miss Helen Merk presided as librarian. She and Miss Josephine were the spinster sisters ot the distinguished Harvard American historian Frederick Merk. They were splendid people, brought up in the intelligent *Frei-Gemeinde* tradition. Miss Josephine was my eighth-grade teacher and I owe her a good deal, a debt that I will presently attempt to acknowledge. I never knew Miss Helen, a mildly formidable personage, as well as the gentler Miss Josephine, but she would listen tolerantly in the library, if no other people were present, to the arguments between

Augie and me. His literary tastes at that stage, I must confess, were more refined than mine. Our arguments always returned to the relative merits of Alexandre Dumas (whom Augie preferred) and Rafael Sabatini (whom I preferred). The chief influence of Dumas on Aug was that he would pepper his conversation with those obvious French exclamations that were left untranslated in the novels. Every other sentence would begin with an explosive "*Mon Dieu!*" (pronounced *Mahn Doo*). Whether Dumas had anything to do with the monocle he was presently sporting, I don't know, or with the gold-plated lorgnette that he acquired and that he would flip out to put down, *de haut en bas*, any whippersnapper who had the temerity to dispute him. He was a great putter-downer, especially of me. I never tried to put him down because he was impervious to the attempt. He had the hide of an elephant in his dogmatic certainties; this, in spite of the fact that when he could afford it a little later, he had made for himself, by the local seamstress, an enormous black velvet cloak lined with bright-green chiffon, a garment he enjoyed putting on over his hefty, naked frame and walking in—stalking in!—at night through the dimly lit back streets of the village. But I am going much too fast. By the time of Aug's black velvet wrap we had read not only "*Dorian Gray*" but Huysmans' "*À rebours*"—real decadents, right there in S.C.H.S.!—although I must say that I have never yearned for a turtle with a jeweled shell laboring about on my living-room floor, the only detail from that silly novel that stays in my mind.

After we became friends, Aug asked me to join his detective organization called the Secret Service Syndicate. The only other member was a shy, shrewd boy named Hugo Schwenker, the son of the local harness maker. Our function was entirely voyeuristic: we were to creep up behind houses with drawn shades and peer in through a possible slit to observe (it was hoped) domestic crises; or follow lovers to the village park and spy upon them in their usually innocent dalliance. The idea was to collect a file of data that could ultimately be used for blackmail, should blackmail prove to be a convenience. Perhaps I need not say that Aug was an avid reader of detective and mystery stories, as he was of horror stories and science fiction. I was a failure in the S.S.S. since I never collected a single damaging item and it became a considerable bore to observe housewives going about their kitchen duties or their husbands dozing over the weekly village newspaper, *The Pioneer Press*. I could have given Aug many items if he had wished to blackmail my parents, but they hardly needed a voyeur.

There were movies in Sauk City on Saturday nights on the second floor of a kind of warehouse, and bossy Augie always got there early, holding two seats at a certain point for himself and me, and one directly in front of his for a girl, Margery, as he called her in his first novel, "Evening in Spring," with whom he professed, and indeed seemed, to be madly in love. His cinematic ideal of feminine beauty was Laura La Plante, who frequently appeared in those silent movies that we saw, and Margery came closer to an approximation of Laura La Plante than any other girl in our high school. She, too, was blond, and she did not have bobbed hair, which Augie despised, but wrapped her long braids around her head like a crown when she put them up. He himself had his own considerable coif by then, an imposing pompadour at least six inches high to which he gave a great deal of attention. What I remember best about Margery is the way she walked, with her pelvis thrust out, a walk uncultivated by any other girl in school. (Later, she must have suffered terrible backaches.) At those Saturday-night movies, while commanding my presence beside him, he was constantly leaning forward, breathing upon her neck, whispering important secrets. Her parents, because of religious differences, he thought, did not want her to be with him, and these movie encounters were among their clandestine meetings. I must have been some sort of foil. Yes, some sort of . . .

One night in spring I was walking with Karl along the dark, elm-tented street in front of the Park Hall. We were a bit high after a visit to the kitchen of the local bootlegger. (Augie was always a teetotaler, and frowned heavily upon our frivolity, as he deemed it.) We met him and Margery, or perhaps they just then came out of the park. There was no doubt some prurient snickering from me, perhaps from both Karl and me. Like King Kong, Aug leaped at me and threw me to the ground in a rage, and I still remember the back of my head hitting the sidewalk. By then we had concrete walks, not boards.

When she was a senior in high school, Margery was, it seems, easily seduced by the high school coach, a young, dark, very sexy-seeming fellow in the then macho style, and Augie, who was no doubt deeply hurt, reviled her as a slut. Later, however, when he wrote his first novel, he softened that crushing experience in a curious way, probably lessening, or trying to, his own pain. Nobody writes novels called "Moon-Calf" any more, but it is really sad, the intensity with which adolescents suffer in life no less than in literature. Or don't they any more? God knows, I did. Pointlessly, one later decides. But that decision is probably mistaken. That silly suffering exudes armor.

I think that by the time Aug got around to writing "Evening in Spring," he had probably got around to putting down his pain. I have just reread it, a curious sentimalization of that town as I remember it. He is quite good on the nature business, the physical atmosphere of the town, especially at night, but wildly false about his own family background as well as very gentle about the end of his relationship with Margery. He always felt it necessary to make up an aristocratic background for his family. (His father was a blacksmith, as was Karl's—curious, the two blacksmiths in that town, their sons my two best friends.) But in Aug's novel (and in some of his later ones) one of the grandfathers is the direct descendant of a very distinguished French nobleman, the whole long name laboriously invented and spelled out; the other grandfather is at least as wise as Thoreau and named, of all names in our almost exclusively German community, Adams.

In that first novel I appear as a shadowy figure named Robin ("with his soft eyes and girlish mouth," the wretch wrote)—as if anyone in Sauk City in 1923 or 1924 would have been caught dead with a son named Robin!

That all came after our joint effort as writers. It must have been in the summer after my first year at the university and before his first year there that we rented an empty cottage hanging over the river for $5 a month, our "office," and became collaborators. For years he had read a magazine called *Weird Tales* and felt that he was an authority on the kind of stories that it published; he had, in fact, already published some stories of his own in that periodical. He persuaded me that I, too, could become a writer, and so we rented that place in that summer and wrote weird tales together. We would discuss a plot; I would write a first draft, and sometimes, at his order, a second; he would then rewrite it; and we would submit the result. We sold quite a number of those stories to *Weird Tales*, being paid anything from $15 to $25 for each, depending on length. Later, Bennett Cerf picked up one of those absurdities for inclusion in his Modern Library volume "*Famous Ghost Stories*," and in the early 1960's, after Aug had established his own little publishing company in Sauk City (Arkham House, Inc., set up largely to bring out book versions of uncollected horror and science-fiction stories, especially the works of H. P. Lovecraft, for whose excessively Latinate prose he had unlimited admiration), he published in book form those weird (in two ways) collaborations of ours in a volume called "*Colonel Markesan and Less Pleasant People*." Some two or three hundred pleasant people are still buying this work each year.

He died too early, and his death left a real hole in my life, even though, in his later years, I no longer saw very much of him. It was a strange friendship, to be sure—part affection, part jealous rivalry on both sides. He was a fantastically prolific writer, and prided himself on his extraordinarily large number of published books in nearly every genre, probably one hundred and fifty volumes when death stopped him. That prolificacy (prolixity?) did not rub off on me. But he was also an extraordinarily disciplined man, and if I picked up any discipline for myself, it came from his example during those trying summer hours in our "office." I thank him for it now. But why don't we tell people these things when they are still alive to hear them?

I'm sure that at some point I did make clear to Miss Josephine Merk how much I felt that I owed her, and it is to her that I would like now briefly to return.

When I left the Sauk City High School, she gave me four books from her own library, all bound in late-Victorian covers, soft engraved leather and such: Milton's Poems, his "Paradise Lost," the Poems of James Russell Lowell, and the Poems of Ralph Waldo Emerson. Each has her name written on the inside cover with an 1890's date. In the Emerson volume she wrote out the final lines of his poem "To J.W." as follows:

Life is too short to waste
In critic peep or cynic bark,
Quarrel or reprimand:
'Twill soon be dark;
Up! mind thine own aim, and
God speed the mark!

With best wishes, always,
Josephine Merk

I don't know if she meant the last word in the Emerson quotation as a pun, but I think that she did.

When she was my teacher she changed my name merely by calling me Mark instead of Marcus, and then presently my friends, my parents, the town went along with that. Later she suggested that when I signed my name, I drop the Robert and even the initial R. and be simply Mark Schorer. Names are mysterious and magical. I think that once I became simply Mark Schorer, I finally knew who I was. I don't think that that younger Marcus Robert (whom I never really knew and don't now, for all my effort to recall him) ever did.

THE
UNWRITTEN
STORY

Quindici anni fa!

These three words were at first a point of reference and then became a kind of joke for Leslie Warden and his wife, Marilyn, in their Italian sojourn. Fifteen years before, in 1955, they had lived in Italy for a year, but except for pauses in Milan and Rome while on their way to other countries, they had not been back since. Now again they were living in Italy for an extended time, and the phrase *quindici anni fa* kept turning up in every kind of conversation, usually to point the contrast between the circumstances of that past time and those of the present. The cost of living, the central heating, the hot baths, the scarcity of maids, the clotted traffic, the frightful new buildings in the cities, television aerials thrusting up from every roof, transistor radios clamped against ears in the streets, in cafés—these and other differences were almost irresistibly marshaled under that verbal banner, and sometimes, after more than six months of it, when either Leslie or Marilyn began a sentence, "*Quindici anni fa* . . ." both would grin sheepishly or even laugh in an embarrassed way, because it was as if they were measuring nearly everything in the world by their petty recollections of fifteen years before.

Nevertheless . . .

Quindici anni fa they had come to know very well this whole group of hill towns—Perugia, Assisi, Arezzo, Orvieto, Gubbio—which they were now revisiting, with Perugia as their *pied-à-terre*. Gubbio, the smallest of them, seemed almost exactly the same, but even there, they felt, the two cold October days of fifteen years before, the wind lashing them furiously with rain, seemed more appropriate to its dour medieval face than the hot, still glare of one day in October now. In Arezzo the great frescoes were half covered for repair and they were all sadly, no, tragically flecked by some damaging rot. In Assisi, they could not find the witch, the *stregone*. In Orvieto, the cathedral supplied the same brilliant shock, but the wine in the restaurants was not as good as they remembered the wine they had once bought for a picnic in the little park that clung to the precipice at the edge of the town. In Perugia the restored Peruginos seemed too bright and the Pisano fountain was not, for Leslie at least, the miracle of delicacy that he had remembered.

Fifteen years before, in the old assistant-professor days, when Leslie was on his first and last academic leave of absence, they had been in Perugia for six weeks to learn Italian in an intensive course at the Università per Stranieri. Even then, at thirty-five, Leslie was a little too old to master another language, and while he went through the motions, he did not really try. But Marilyn, who was six years younger, who was always more conscientious than he, and who felt that she should present a good example of study habits to their daughter Barbara, then ten years old and traveling with them, worked hard at the language and did very well. Since then she had kept it up, had taken adult-education conversation courses and a course in Dante, had plowed through *I Promessi Sposi* during much of one winter, regularly read new works of fiction by popular Italian writers, a few of whom she had managed to meet—Moravia, Silone, Vittorini, Calvino, and so on—and in the past few years she had had a subscription to *Tempo Presente*. Now she was fluent in the language, and she could only feel impatience with Leslie's bumbling "pig Italian," as she called it, and the look of stupid incomprehension that crept over his face when some tradesman or waiter or public servant blasted out a question of more than ten words. If Leslie attempted an entire sentence, it was grotesquely ungrammatical—but he rarely did. His Italian consisted in the main of a packet of phrases—*quindici anni fa!*—that he sprinkled through his English. It was all the more absurd that he should have adopted an air of sentimental proprietorship over Italy and things Italian.

They were nearly at the end of their projected two weeks in Perugia. One morning in their rooms in the Brufani Palace, after they had finished their coffee and Leslie was standing on a balcony in his pajamas, looking down at the square through his heavy horn-rimmed glasses, he said, "Come here. Look at the sunshine. How summer stays! It's that special Umbrian gold in early autumn."

Marilyn knew about "that special gold of Umbria," he had told her before, and, when, wrapping her dressing gown around her, she joined him, she looked up at the sky, which was perhaps a special blue, and at the billowing beige clouds. It *was* lovely! Far away, across the deep-blue morning valley, Assisi gleamed and shimmered as though it were made of silver and glass.

"Let's go to Trasimeno today," he said.

She was not enthusiastic. "Why?"

"Why?"

"Yes. I think I've about had it, you know."

"Had what?"

"Well, 'that special gold of Umbria,' among other things."

She turned back into the room and at the dressing table began vigorously to brush her hair. He watched her. It was reddish-blond hair that had some attractive streaks of gray in it now, and she combed it in exactly the way she had then, rather short and straight back from her rounded forehead and her fine delicate temples. With the high hairline her profile was almost like a Piero head, or that Pollaiuolo in the Poldi Pezzoli.

"I don't care if it's today or tomorrow," he said, "but I do want to go back there before we leave."

"But why?"

"It was one of the perfect days of our lives that we had there."

"Your life perhaps."

"Yours, too. We could swim again. It's a perfect day. And maybe with the reminder, I can write that story yet. I've always wanted to."

"You've told it too many times," she said.

"Maybe not. Give it a chance!"

"Very well," she agreed at last and kept on brushing. He could see her pale lips move a little as she counted the strokes.

He went into his room to dress, and smiled. There were some differences! Standing in his shower, he thought of that time fifteen years ago when the three of them had lived in a *pensione* beyond the walls of the town; because the *padrona* had made such a fuss about heating up water for baths, they had developed the habit of renting a room for an hour at the Brufani, which was then one of the few places in town that had running hot water, taking their baths, and departing again. Now they were staying there—

he was walking around his bedroom, dripping water and trailing an enormous thick towel—staying there, with two baths, and these two tall, handsome rooms overlooking the Carducci gardens. "*Quindici anni fa!*" he heard himself exclaim, even as he wondered why, since the excursion generally had been so disappointing, he felt so happy.

"What?" Marilyn called.

"Nothing."

"I thought you said something."

"No, nothing," he said as he came into her room in his shorts, raising his arms to pull on his shirt. She looked at him in quick appraisal. Even at fifty there was something neat and almost boyish about his figure. She wondered sometimes how he managed it, living such a generally soft life—that life to which he had been freed by a not entirely unexpected inheritance, freed even of the mild routines of the not entirely brilliant beginning of an academic career in Beloit, Wisconsin, freed to live almost entirely as he pleased, to travel much, to write a little. His waist, with no bulge whatever, still measured thirty-two, while hers was now twenty-eight. She frowned. He was standing behind her, and bent over her to kiss the top of her head. "I'm glad we're going," he said.

"I hope you won't be disappointed again," she said lightly, on the way to her bath.

He was dressed before she was and stood on the balcony off her room in his youthful clothes, his buckskin desert boots, his yellow linen slacks from Brooks, and his pale-blue pullover with a dark-blue and yellow scarf inside the open collar, a checked cotton jacket over his arm. In that morning light you could not tell if his hair was blond or gray—it was both, of course, but mostly gray. Now he was wearing his other glasses, identical frames with dark lenses, and looking down approvingly at the roof of his Mercedes, parked immediately before the hotel, its planes gleaming in the sun and being made to gleam more by a boy from the hotel who was lovingly rubbing it with a cloth. That was a difference, too. On that other October day so long ago there had been five of them, all crowded into a second-hand Fiat owned by a girl named Peggy. He had forgotten Peggy's last name. She, too, was studying Italian at the university, and from someone later he had heard that she had married a bearded Irishman and lived in Paris, but they had never seen her again. Then there were Marilyn and Barbara and himself and a poet from Northwestern named John, also a student, whose poems Leslie still saw occasionally in the periodicals but whom he had not encountered again since that time. A pleasant fellow, and where are the snows? Now Barbara was twenty-five, working in the offices of a fashion magazine on Madison Avenue, living attractively in her apartment on East Eighty-first Street. And today he and Marilyn would drive alone in the Mercedes to swim again in Lake Trasimeno. *Quindici anni fa* . . .

"Ready?" Marilyn asked behind him.

She was wearing a severely cut green linen suit that brought out a glint of green in her gray eyes, and she had tied a white chiffon scarf around her head, and she had on high-heeled white pumps. She never wore low heels, even when they were climbing around the tortured streets and byways of these hill towns, and she had never owned a pair of flats. It was true enough that heels emphasized her elegantly high instep and made her fine long legs look longer, but such shoes were not practical, and this habit or even principle of hers did not accord with what he regarded as her serious scholarly side. In one white-gloved hand she held the cords of the white plastic bag that contained their beach things. He opened the door into the corridor and took the bag as she passed him.

He drove, and intermittently on the way they talked about that other time. "Do you think there's a chance of finding that boatman?" he asked.

"Mario," she said.

"Not Mario! His name was Fausto, don't you remember? Mario's the waiter in Florence."

"Oh, yes, Fausto."

"It was you who found that out, just by accident, and it was only because we knew his name that we got your watch back."

"Of course. He said very little, but at one point he asked Barbie, '*Come ti chiami?*' and after she told him, I asked him, just to be friendly, '*Come si chiama?*' and he said, 'Fausto.' It seemed like such an appropriate name for a boatman, somehow. Or am I thinking of Charon?"

"Good God, not Charon!"

"Carone, the Italians say. No, I don't suppose that that would be a possible proper name."

"I hope not."

That day! The five of them piling out of the crowded little Fiat on the waterfront of that town. He could not remember its name now. Neither of them had thought of that. Marilyn dug into the plastic bag for the faithful Michelin, which this time failed her. Then she opened up a road map and presently said, "It must be Passignano. That seems to be the only town on the lake on this highway. And there seem to be three islands in the lake, none of them called Isola Bella, as I remembered. There's Minore, Maggiore, and Polvese."

"Isola Maggiore, that's it!"

"Not Isola Bella?"

"No. Maggiore." He glanced at her for a second, and said, "It's more like me than like you to remember that island as Isola Bella."

"Yes. It is."

That island! One of them, probably Peggy, had heard of a small hotel, only ten or fifteen rooms, on that island, where one could lunch attractively in the garden, under the trees. Both John and Leslie had supplied themselves with large bottles of brandy before they left Perugia, and there had been some morning tippling during the drive, and now the two men had what seemed to them, at least, a hilarious time haggling with the men clustered near their boats on the shore about the price of a trip to the island and back. Finally they settled on the one called Fausto, a sturdy fellow who looked about twenty-five and who agreed to take them over then and pick them up again at six o'clock, five hundred lire each way. They crowded into his little boat, he pulled the cord on the outboard motor, surprisingly enough it started at once, and they were putt-putting away over that strange water the color of a cloudy, pale-green opal.

Then there was the island itself, the charming little hotel among the big trees, the spirited signora who managed it, an English lady staying there, her friend, and a young woman from the island who made elaborate lace and sold Peggy a blouse of it. A swim, lunch under the trees, arrangements to meet the two ladies in Assisi next day to consult the male witch they knew about there, naps on blankets in the shaded grass after all the cold white wine, another swim in the soft water, this time without suits, the nips at the brandy bottles all through the day, the euphoria deepening and swelling, the sun sinking, the wind rising, the lake choppy, Fausto returning in the twilight . . .

"You don't have to brake that way on every curve," Marilyn's clipped voice said, yanking him out of his dream.

"You've told me that for years."

"But you don't! It's so simple. Just slow up a little before you come into the curve, then—"

"I know. Look, dear, let me drive the way I always drive."

She sighed and lifted her hand to her face. Out of the corner of his eye he saw the gold of her wristwatch flash in the sun, the watch that had brought on the climax of that day.

She had had it for less than a year. It was his present to her on their tenth wedding anniversary. It had cost five hundred dollars, which was a lot of money for them in those days. It had a fine tiny mechanism embedded in a rather heavy gold bracelet that clipped onto her wrist. After Fausto had helped them out of the boat and they had paid him his thousand lire and he had gone away and they were settled briefly in a café on the main street of the town, Marilyn discovered that she had lost it. Then there was a great flurry of excitement, telephone calls back to the island, a hurried search there, no watch, perhaps tomorrow . . . but then Marilyn had another thought: in the boat on the way back, when the wind blew so crisply, she had hugged Barbie to her and bundled her, with herself, into the cape she was wearing, and in that tangle of folds, didn't she have a sensation of the watch slipping off her wrist? Then the boat must be found! Where was—? *Fausto!*

Half the village, it seemed, helped them to find him where he lived, and then with much babbling they were all running through the dark streets back to the waterfront, and Fausto picked out his boat from the row of them that were beached there, and in the darkness they searched it, and finally lifted the duckboards in the bottom of the boat, and there, believe it or not, under one of them was the watch! Everyone, villagers and all, shouted in triumph. It seemed nothing less than miraculous. Leslie gave Fausto another thousand lire, and John and Leslie finished the brandy in elation. Even Marilyn, who hated the stuff, had a swallow of it with them, and then coughed and gagged for five minutes until they found her a glass of water. And the long drive back through the soft darkness, no one talking much, and Leslie happily drunk. He glanced at Marilyn beside him, staring straight ahead: perhaps it was his drinking that day that caused her to remember it somewhat less happily than he did.

They knew at once that Passignano was indeed the town as the Mercedes wound down into it from the hills. At first everything seemed the same as it had fifteen years before—the opalescent water lying still in the sun, the tidy tree-lined shore, the village stretched along the main street and piled up for a short distance on the hills behind it. Leslie parked the car beside the chief café, where they had discovered the loss of the watch, and they got out and crossed the street together. Then they began to notice the differences. The shore where the little boats used to be was empty. A very solid-looking new pier stretched out into the lake and at the end of it a new-looking white excursion launch was moored. At the end of the pier, too, was a small glassed-in ticket office and on a post beside it, a framed *orario*. They walked out and found the office empty and locked, and they studied the schedule. Apparently the next sailing was at twelve, and it was only eleven. The boat made the whole round of the lake: Passignano, Isola Minore, Isola Maggiore, Castiglione, on the opposite shore, Isola Polvese, Passignano again.

"That's the island," said Leslie, looking out over the water. "Isola Maggiore."

It loomed mistily before them, muted greens and blues and tawny blurs. One end was dominated by a fortress-like castle, high up. "I don't remember the castle, do you?" asked Leslie.

"I think so."

"Strange. I don't. Well, what should we do?"

"Do you want to wait an hour?"

"Let's see if we can't get our own boat, perhaps even find Fausto."

They went back to the café, and when the young woman who was in charge approached them as they came tentatively in under the arbor in front of the place, Marilyn asked her if it was possible to rent a boat.

Perhaps, but for that they must go to the beach, which was up the street, and inquire there.

Did the lady by any chance know a man named Fausto?

"Fausto!" she exclaimed. "Without doubt."

Marilyn explained that fifteen years before a man named Fausto had taken them to Isola Maggiore.

"Wait a moment!" She called into the bar, and when a young boy in a white shirt appeared, she gave him a rapid order that was incomprehensible to Leslie. Marilyn explained. "She's dispatched him to get Fausto. He apparently has a shop nearby, a *negozio*."

"It's too unlikely that he's the same one," Leslie said. "Certainly ours had no shop."

"But there can't be more than one man here with that name."

"Seat yourselves please," the young woman said. "He'll come in a moment, if he's there."

And in little more than a minute, in fact, the young boy in the white shirt was walking briskly back into the arbor, and behind him came a man, presumably their Fausto, more slowly, looking quizzical, and the color of a chestnut. He was wearing the same or the same kind of costume that their Fausto had worn—sandals, a pair of those bright-blue shorts worn by many Italian workers in the summer, under them, no doubt, swimming trunks, and a sleeveless undershirt of jersey mesh. He stood before them, and Marilyn took over.

"You are Fausto?"

"Sì."

"*Quindici anni fa—*" she began, and told him how he

had taken them and three others to Isola Maggiore in his boat, how they had had lunch there in the little hotel, how he had come back for them at six, how she had lost her watch, how they had summoned him, and how they had found it in the bottom of his boat.

He hesitated. When he spoke he allowed that fifteen years was a long time. He wasn't certain that he remembered. He studied them speculatively.

Could he take them over again today?

Ah, but he no longer had a boat. Things were different. Many things had changed. There was the big boat, leaving in less than an hour.

But weren't there any small boats anywhere?

His face brightened as he studied Marilyn. Wait! He had a *collega* who owned a boat. Perhaps the colleague would rent it. Would they come up to the beach with him?

"A moment, please," Marilyn then said, and to Leslie, "It's certainly he, isn't it?"

"I'm sure."

"If things have changed so," she asked Fausto, "can we still have lunch on the island?"

"*Sì, sì.*"

"In the little hotel, with the pleasant signora?"

No, the hotel was no longer a hotel, but there was a small chalet on the other side of the island where they could eat, and as for the signora, she happened to be sitting right there, and he nodded at a table behind the Wardens. They turned to look and now there was no question whatever: certainly they beheld the signora in the woman sitting so erect in her dark-red dress, her black hair pulled up high from the handsome round face, talking so animatedly to an old villager with a gray beard and a faded beret who shared the table with her.

"It's too good to be true!" said Leslie.

"*Che coincidenza!*" exclaimed Fausto.

"I must speak to her," Marilyn said, and approached her, saying tentatively, "Signora . . ."

The signora turned her head slowly. "*Sì?*"

"Signora . . ."

"*Mi dica*, signora."

Marilyn began again. "*Quindici anni fa . . .*" and as the story came out once more, the signora's face brightened and she was saying, "*Sì, sì, sì,*" and Marilyn said, "And there was an English lady—"

Ah, yes! Signora Graham. She no longer came to Passignano, but sometimes she came to visit her in her villa on the road to Perugia.

And did she remember meeting them in Assisi next day, and the visit to the *stregone*?

But of course she remembered! And when they finally found his house, it was after the hour of Santa Maria, and he would not summon up any spirits from the dead because at that hour it was most dangerous. He had told their fortunes with playing cards.

Yes. But he was no longer there, in Assisi. At any rate, a few days before they had hunted for him without success.

The signora had heard nothing of him for some years. Perhaps he was dead. Even fifteen years ago, he was very old—did not the signora remember?

Yes, yes. But then what of the young woman who made the splendid lace?

Ah, did they remember how much she had wanted to be married? Well, she had been married many years now, and had children so tall and so tall and so, and this old gentleman was her father.

The old villager beamed at the strangers, and Marilyn hastily summarized the interchange for Leslie, for whom it had gone much too fast.

And the *ragazza bionda*, the signora asked, *carina, carissima*, what had become of her?

Oh, she was splendid, grown of course, a "career woman"—carefully enunciated in English—in New York. No, she was not married.

"*Quindici anni fa*," the signora mused with a soft smile.

Fausto moved up and said to the signora that fifteen years ago he had taken them to the island in his boat, and today he was to do so again, if he found a boat.

Marilyn spoke again. Even if the hotel was no longer operating, they could still swim there, at the little beach?

Oh no. The beach, too, was a ruin now. *Brutto, brutto!*

"But I will find you a good place," Fausto quickly said.

"*Forse*, Fausto! Perhaps, perhaps."

"*Sì, sì*, signora!"

"*Va bene*, Fausto."

Then there was a rush of friendly farewells and much hope that less than fifteen years would pass before the signori came again to Trasimeno, and the signora was nodding in a stately way and the old one beaming while he seemed to shake gently all over in a kind of palsy. Fausto turned away, and as the Wardens followed him, Marilyn explained to Leslie everything that had been said. "It does not sound so good," she concluded.

"Oh, yes," he said blithely. "It'll be fine. It's all going so amazingly! First Fausto, then the signora, then even the lacemaker's old father! Look at the lake, the olive-covered hills. Everything soft. Peace, peace, peace, The guidebook says it's heart-shaped."

"Dreamer," said Marilyn as they arrived at the squalid public beach, where flimsy cabins in need of paint seemed to reel in the sun in a ragged row, faded umbrellas flapped in the breeze, and children and dogs disported themselves noisily on the dark littered sand and the water's edge. Fausto had engaged an old man in conversation by the time the Wardens were stepping through the sand. This was the *collega*, apparently the administrator of the beach, and from the way that he swayed in the sun, apparently a little drunk. As the Wardens approached, Fausto seemed to be contemplating Marilyn's legs, and it was as if with an effort that he looked up and said that the colleague would let them have his boat until four o'clock for four thousand lire. Very good. And would Fausto come back for them at three? Fausto would stay with them if he might. Oh? He was not needed in the *negozio*, where his brother was on duty. Was it good? Oh, very good!

Without more discussion, Fausto took off his sandals and pulled down his shorts, and for a moment he stood there in his now rather absurd undershirt, not quite meeting the top of a yellow bikini. The muscles of his short legs made them seem nearly columnar, in a Doric way. His shoulders were broad, his chest deep. At the line across his hips the top of the bikini cut into what was just the beginning of the inevitable pasta roll. Most extraordinary was his color, nearly mahogany. He smiled with questioning interest, friendliness, only a little deference. He could have done with a shave.

Abruptly, as if he had just said, "Well, there I am!" he bundled his sandals and shorts together and began to wade out in the shallow water to a boat in need of paint, untied it from its buoy, and began to push it in to a low wall at the end of the beach. The owner knelt unsteadily on the edge of the wall to hold the boat while Fausto arranged some old canvas-covered pillows in the prow and then stood up to give first Marilyn, then Leslie his strong hand as they stepped down. When they were settled, the owner gave the boat a shove, and as it drifted away from the wall, Fausto pulled the cord on the outboard motor and it chugged to life. He steered a careful course out through the young swimmers, and just after he had cleared them all, the motor died.

Unperturbed, Fausto worked at the motor—pulled the cord a few times without success, fingered the choke, pulled again, unscrewed the cap on the tank, peered in, blew in, pulled again, and the thing would cough uncertainly but never cough itself into life. Fausto was perspiring from his effort, and with an exasperated gesture he pulled his undershirt off and wiped his face with it. The boat, meanwhile, was drifting back toward the shore among the swimmers.

"This is probably the end of our excursion," Marilyn remarked. But then they saw a larger boat than theirs detaching itself from a group at the shore and come chugging out toward them. It was the kind of boat that fishermen use to bring in the haul from their nets—shaped almost like a gondola in the prow, flat and broad in the midsection, squared off in the stern, where a motor was manned by a boy of seventeen or eighteen. He circled Fausto's boat and they shouted some guttural exchanges, not words but strange animal sounds, and then, bringing his boat very close, the boy leaned over and seized the rope fastened to Fausto's prow. With that in his hand, he towed the drifting boat back out into the open water. There was more of that grunting communication, now with gestures from Fausto. The boy did not look Italian. He had light-brown hair, sharply cut features, a clear Nordic beauty.

"He must be a Dane or something," Leslie said, "and they have no common language."

The grunts and gestures had served as well, for now the boy was handing Fausto a screwdriver and a pair of pliers, and then, idling his motor, sat back and watched as Fausto removed the motor from the planking, unscrewed the gas cap, stood and lifted the motor up with him, and then turned it over and let the gasoline pour into the lake. Standing up in the boat with his legs spread for balance, his pelvis thrust forward and his back arched, holding the heavy motor up and out with the flexed power of his arms,

the brown figure looked, for the moment and in a comic
way, Herculean. When the tank was empty, he eased it
down on the planking and secured it. Then he pulled a
large plastic container from under the seat and refilled the
tank. To Marilyn he explained—as she explained to Leslie—
that his *collega* was a drunken old slob who didn't keep his
motor clean. She looked away from both Fausto and Leslie
at the nearly naked brown boy in the boat that still attended theirs.

"He's the most beautiful thing I've ever seen," she
said.

"Thank God for his pliers," said Leslie.

"He is *so* beautiful!"

"Like many Danes. Or even an occasional German."

Fausto started up his motor without difficulty, and,
waving to the boy, steered out into the lake. Then Marilyn
called to him, "That boy—is he a foreigner?"

No, no. From Passignano.

But what was wrong with him, with his language?

Deaf and dumb since birth, said Fausto.

"*Il poverino!*"

"*Ma molto intelligente!*"

"*Ma! Poverino, poverino,*" she murmured, and to Leslie, "Deaf and dumb since birth."

"And I thought he was a Dane or at least a German!"

"The language barrier takes many forms, doesn't it?"
she asked. "Do you understand Fausto at all? Have you
noticed that he uses *voi* instead of the polite form? In the
Mussolini period they tried to reform the language. Get rid
of *Lei!* No nonsense about formal linguistic manners, *il
cerimoniale!* Everyone equal, ha!"

Leslie did not answer because he was confused by his
wife's sudden agitation, and then, as he hesitated, because
Fausto, who had been studying the Wardens quizzically as
they sat there together in the prow, was suddenly laughing

loudly and calling to Marilyn that now indeed he did remember that day *quindici anni fa,* because he had suddenly remembered the two gentlemen sitting together in the boat and exchanging a bottle of cognac.

This Leslie understood and he felt very happy. Remembering the trade name of that harsh brandy that they then drank, he shouted back to Fausto, "*Sì! Sì!* Buton! Buton!"

"*Sì!*" cried Fausto. "Buton!" And now, he called, he remembered it all very clearly, the entire party, and the day ending with the episode of the watch. The two men laughed together across the space between them, and Leslie waved to Fausto at his end of the boat, shouting "Buton!" happily. But that was almost the last happy moment for Leslie.

After that, everything became rather dull and sometimes plain boring. Fausto, such a silent young man, had developed into a positively garrulous older one, and his observations, which threatened constantly to become lectures, were necessarily directed to Marilyn rather than to Leslie, and Marilyn, as the time passed, gave Leslie briefer and briefer summaries, until at last they were quite perfunctory.

First there was the problem of the lake. For many years the water level had been sinking, and while this made pleasant beaches and brought many tourists, it also threatened the abundance of fish, the chief livelihood of the villagers. Then under the Fanfani government water was piped in over the surrounding hills, and the lake was restored to the level that it had once enjoyed, but the signori could see that the shores, both of the mainland and of the islands, had been ruined, and now no tourists came in great numbers. The villagers who had made their living by transporting tourists about the lake now owned fishing boats and nets. He himself had a shop and, with his brother, made and sold tackle.

Leslie studied the shore as the boat progressed doggedly toward the island. He had not noticed earlier that it was lined everywhere with a thick growth of rushes and that here and there among the rushes stood dead trees, gaunt and black and bare, *brutto, brutto,* as the lady said.

It was sad about the beaches and the tourists, Fausto agreed, but the villages on the lake were now more prosperous than they had been for many years. He gave the number of fish, in the millions or billions, that were taken from the lake each year, and he named the chief varieties: *lasche, tinche, lucci, carpe, anguille.*

Raising her voice over the putt-putt of the motor, Marilyn asked, "*Ma,* Fausto, *quanta gente vi abita addesso* . . . ?" How many people now live on the several islands, with the altered situation? And they were off again on one of their statistical exchanges that left Leslie to study the overgrown shores of Isola Maggiore, which they were beginning to skirt. Fausto seemed to be searching for a place to beach his boat without breaking through one of the many nets that were stretched between stakes jutting out of the water just beyond the edge of the rushes along the shore. His nautical efforts, Leslie observed a little sourly to himself, did not make him less talkative.

Even as he beached the boat in an inlet between nets and rushes, he was telling Marilyn about St. Francis's famous forty days of Lenten prayers with nothing to eat except—as Leslie got it—the little fish that kept flapping up into his hands and which he kept tossing back into the water, saying, "No, no, bless you, little brother, bless you." So how did he eat any if he kept throwing them all back? Leslie wondered, while Fausto continued talking. On this very rock toward which they were now scrambling over the stony shore—Marilyn, thank heaven, without her shoes, which she had left in the boat—St. Francis spent his forty days of trial. And there, please observe, signori, in that crevice, is a wooden statue of St. Francis, *Seicento*, now much decayed, the paint faded, to commemorate his long trial and fast. Fausto laughed. The ants kept eating it, and every now and then some islander took it down and held it in the water for a while, to discourage the ants. Marilyn laughed with Fausto and then explained to Leslie about the ants. Leslie laughed.

Fausto laughed, and with a flurry of gestures indicated that he had decided to be an islander. He approached the wooden figure, perhaps four feet tall, and, easily lifting it off its pedestal, put it over his shoulder and marched back to the water's edge. Stepping carefully into the lake, he lowered the statue until he had it in his arms, like a large baby, then got it down into his hands and, with a satirically pious look, plunged it under the surface of the water and held it there in a kind of violence, as if he were drowning it. He grinned over his shoulder. "Death to all ants!" he said to Marilyn. Presently he lifted the figure, streaming water, out of the lake, and unceremoniously returned it to its pedestal, still laughing.

Leslie looked at the dripping statue, a recognizably human figure although nearly featureless and striated with decay, its painted surface a blur of faded reds and blues. He found himself wondering whether it might be possible to buy the statue from someone. Properly restored and mounted, it could be very striking in their foyer, smack in front of the floor-length mirror. He asked Marilyn to ask Fausto, but she gave him only an impatient smile and asked instead if it was here that they were to swim.

Sì, sì. And if the signori would be so good as to walk around the rock, they would find a place where they could comfortably change into their bathing costumes.

Leslie stared dubiously, almost glumly, at the rushes that grew from the water and at the cluttered shore, stones and broken bottles and a few rusted cans, driftwood, no sand whatever. "Well, it's hardly ideal," he said, "but here we are, so let's try it. Watch where you step."

When they came out from behind the rock in their swimming suits, they saw that Fausto was already in the water, standing beyond the rushes, the water up to his waist, his back to them. Something in his posture suggested to Leslie that he was urinating but he repressed the impulse to say so to Marilyn, and when presently Fausto dove ahead into the water and struck out, there was nothing to do but follow. Gingerly, walking on submerged, slippery, moss-covered rocks, they made their way through the rushes until the water lapped at their thighs; then they plunged into it and swam to Fausto, who was lashing about with aimless gusto. But there was nothing exhilarating about this warm and sluggish water, nothing like that other time. After ten minutes of desultory paddling about, Leslie said, "Let's give it up," and they went back to the shore to dress. When they came from behind the rock, Fausto, in his undershirt, was waiting beside the boat and helped them in. Once Marilyn was seated, she ran a comb through her hair, covered it again with her white scarf, and pushed her feet into her high-heeled shoes. The motor chugged to life and the boat moved slowly out through the rushes and the nets into the open water.

For about a hundred yards Fausto stayed as close to the shore as he easily could and then suddenly shut off his motor. He pointed to a wide break in the rushes and said, *"Ecco l'albergo."*

The hotel was a ruin, neglected and obviously uninhabited for years, with a great hole in its roof, a ragged wound, the once white paint now gray and scaling, windows broken, shutters sagging. It stood among rotting trees in what was nearly a swamp, and here and there bedraggled chickens scratched about in the mud. Marilyn gasped, "Oh, how sad!" and Leslie said, "God!" The sight so depressed him as he stared at it that he now made no attempt at all to understand Fausto's Italian as he launched into another lecture and started up his motor again. While the boat moved toward the southern end of the island, Fausto kept pointing upward, as if to take their thoughts away from what was below, and even the inattentive Leslie could understand that he was talking about the castle, whose crenelated ramparts they could see in glimpses above the foliage of trees that crowned the heights of the island. Fausto slowed down the boat to show them a channel cut into the shore and leading to a dock at the foot of a road that wound up into the wooded slopes, all this being the access to the castle, and then he began his explanations, *castello* this, *castello* that, and they putt-putted on around the end of the island and started up the length of its farther shore.

Marilyn gave Leslie a summarized history of the castle. In ancient times a monastery, it became the property of a wealthy family named Guglielmi di Vulci in the nineteenth century—how relentlessly she adored exact details! Leslie thought—and this family built the imposing residence, called Villa Isabella, on the old foundations. In the Fascist years it was appropriated by the government and became the seat of political conferences and convocations, then after the war it reverted to its owners; but now that family was reduced to a single old lady who came for only a few weeks each summer and possessed herself of only a few of the many rooms. At the moment no one was in residence, she concluded, and when she stopped speaking, Fausto immediately took up again. He was reminded of the war years and of the time of the German occupation, when they completely controlled the life of his village. Politically they were of course impossible, but for their skill in administration, in organization, their efficiency with machines, for all this he had great admiration.

Some of this Leslie understood, and he muttered to Marilyn, "Good God, do we need this wisdom?"

"Let him talk," Marilyn murmured.

But Fausto had stopped talking and was attending now only to the boat, which he turned sharply in order to bring it up alongside a dock that projected into the water from a little country piazza a few feet higher than the level of the lake. Here, Fausto indicated, they could have their lunch.

It looked pleasant enough. There were a few tables and benches under the trees where a half dozen men were lounging, and there were two buildings, one an octagonal affair, mostly windows, that advertised local crafts, the other a shabby little cottage that proved to be Fausto's chalet. When they came to the shop, Leslie saw that it was locked up and that the local crafts seemed to consist entirely of some undistinguished ceramic objects and lace doilies of various sizes; there was no sign of anything so interesting or elegant as Peggy's blouse of fifteen years ago. The chalet was open, for a young woman in an apron came out and greeted Fausto as they approached. He explained that they would like to eat and she told him what was available and suggested that they sit down at the one table that was empty. Fausto casually greeted the men idling at the other tables and told the Wardens that these were fishermen at their midday rest. Then he returned to his reminiscences of the German occupation, but after only a few sentences, one of the men nearest him suddenly interrupted.

"Yes, and what did you do?" It sounded like a jibe.

Fausto stared back at him, and then without an answer shifted his position so that his back was turned to the men and he could talk without being overheard by them.

"What did you do, Fausto?" Marilyn asked.

He grimaced with mild impatience and explained that he had been a boy, too young for military service, and when the Germans came, he worked for them as a mechanic, and so he was in a position to say that he respected their machines and their handling of machines.

Leslie's attention wandered again. He looked at the men sprawled at the several tables around them. They were all quite old, all sitting there in their undershirts, like Fausto, but, with their lank arms and hollow chests and skinny, leathery necks, very unlike him. They were also anything but talkative. A few of them were drinking beer, but there was no conviviality; they looked depressed, and they depressed Leslie. Like the hotel, they were ruins of the island, itself ruined. They had none of the gentility or grace that old men, old age can have, but were merely worn out, the exhausted, tattered products of hard and wasted lives, wasted themselves, bleak. They made him uneasy, stolidly staring at him and Marilyn, and he wished that he were wearing other clothes. He wished that they would go. And when the waitress came with a gingham cloth and some cutlery to prepare their table, the men did begin to drift away, as if they, too, were uncomfortable, two of them down to the dock, where they got into a boat, the others up a cobbled path that disappeared under the trees behind the weathered shack of a restaurant.

Their lunch consisted of tasteless soft spaghetti, thin tough steak, and rather warm beer. The cheese, like the bread, was very hard, and the only available fruit was a bowl of mealy yellow apples. Fausto devoted himself to this fare with a gusty satisfaction that neither Marilyn nor Leslie could share or emulate, but Marilyn, at any rate, was polite in her continued expression of interest in the affairs of the island, the lake, the town on the shore. Leslie brooded, looking grumpy, and asked for more beer when the young woman came to see if she could bring them anything.

They sat there for what seemed to him like a long

time, and Marilyn would glance quickly at the disconsolate Leslie before plying Fausto with another question that elicited another spate of information and extended their pointless sitting. There was more information on the fishing industry, statistics about employment and unemployment, talk about the life and the prospects of village young people, talk about Fausto's enterprises, his successful shop, and the failure of the ceramics industry that he and his brother had attempted; talk, apparently, even about his private life, his contented bachelor state, and then more talk about the *castello*. Fausto stood up. Would the signori not like to see the *castello*? It was not a long climb.

Marilyn accepted the invitation with what seemed to Leslie a nearly perverse eagerness. He said that he himself did not feel like even a little climbing and why didn't they go without him? He would stay here, drink another beer, settle the check, and be waiting for them when they came back.

"Very well," said Marilyn, "there's no point in your going if it doesn't interest you." She stood up. "*Va bene, Fausto. Andiamo—solamente io e Lei.*"

He looked surprised, glanced dubiously at Leslie, shrugged, and said, "*Se voi volete*, signora," and the two of them went down to the dock, Fausto leading. Leslie watched him help her step into the boat, start his motor, and maneuver the boat away from the dock and out into the lake. He signaled to the waitress, who was standing in the door of the restaurant observing, and asked for another beer and *il conto*. He tried to explain that the others had gone to the castle and that he would wait for them here. Before she returned with his beer and the check, the sound of Fausto's motor had died away. Leslie paid the check, thanked the woman, and poured his beer. As he drank it slowly in the placid semi-shade, he found himself thinking of the deaf-mute who had provided the pliers. What would happen to him, who heard no words and knew none to speak if he could speak, as, aging in this place, he, too, turned into an old man with stringy arms, hollow chest, wrinkled neck, the prisoner of an endless silence? Nothingness, nothingness . . . Leslie grew sleepy, and presently, his beer only half finished, he put his head down on his arms and was dozing.

It was the cough-cough of Fausto's motor that woke him. They were coming into the dock again. He looked at his watch and saw that they had been gone for about an hour. He stood up, feeling fuzzy and thick-headed, and started down to the boat, from which Marilyn was waving to him.

"How was it?" he asked her as he settled beside her, and yawned. "Sorry. I've been napping."

"Mildly interesting," she said, and Fausto once more took the boat out into the lake. "We walked part way around the walls and got into the main courtyard, but there seemed to be no attendant around to show us more."

Looking back from where they now were in the lake, they could see the walls of the castle and their occasional squat towers. "Is it interesting architecture at all?"

"Not really. We were able to get up into one of those towers. The view was pretty."

"I didn't miss much, I take it."

"No," she said, and smiled at him.

"Our friend seems to have talked himself out," Leslie said, looking at Fausto.

"Doesn't he!"

Fausto was giving his entire attention to the water ahead of him while he made the straightest possible approach to Passignano. The pale-green water was without a ripple, not at all like that other choppy return, and the air was mild and yielding, soft as pollen.

"All rather disappointing," Leslie said, and yawned again. "I can't shake my sleepiness," he said.

"These attempts usually are. I tried to warn you."

"Oh, well . . . Nothing lost."

They joined Fausto in his silence and watched the village take on its features, out of the misty air, as the boat approached the beach. Fausto reduced his speed and then cut off his motor as the boat went smoothly to the seawall, where the old man was kneeling, his arm extended to seize the prow. Leslie tossed the rope up to him, Fausto leaped agilely out and bent to give his hand to Marilyn. *"Ecco,"* he said.

Leslie handed up their beach bag and climbed out after Marilyn. The old man was tying up the boat. Now the beach was largely shadowed, but a half dozen children were still running about among the same miscellany of dogs, and a few dark heads still bobbed in the water. Marilyn's eyes were searching the end of the beach where the boats were. "The deaf-mute," she said. "I would like to see him again. He means something to me—no language, young, so beautiful, and without a language, probably in some way unknown to us without a *world.* I can't bear it. Do you see him?"

"No. I've been thinking about him, too."

Her eyes were blurred with tears. "Fausto," she cried in agitation, *"il giovanotto sordomuto— Lui è qui?"*

Fausto studied the boats and consulted his colleague. Then he said, *"No,* signora, *è partito. Dove non lo so. Ma— perchè?"*

She answered in English and answered to Leslie, "He meant something to me. It's too sad to bear!"

Leslie turned to Fausto and pulled his engagement book, together with his wallet, from his breast pocket. He opened the engagement book to an empty page and gave it to Marilyn with his pen. "Let's get his whole name this time. Will you ask him to write it down?"

"Why?"

"We'll send him a Christmas card or something."

She turned to Fausto and made the request. He took

the book and then with what seemed like great labor wrote in it and returned the book and pen to Leslie. The writing was crabbed and Leslie was not sure of his reading. "Cavallare?" he asked.

"*Sì, sì*, signor."

"*Grazie*, Fausto. *Allora*." He opened his wallet. "*Quatromila per il Suo collega . . . E . . .*" Leslie looked thoughtfully at his wallet and at Fausto. "*E anche duemila per Lei?*"

"Signor, *non è necessario*."

Leslie pressed two more notes into his hand with the others. "*E grazie molto*, Fausto."

"*Grazie voi*, signor!"

Marilyn abruptly intervened. The money, she protested, could not possibly repay his kindness, for which they were most grateful. Ah, but he had enjoyed their company very much and was likewise most grateful.

Leslie picked up the beach bag. He looked at his wristwatch. "*Dobbiamo andare*," he ventured. "*Arrivederci*, Fausto."

"*Arrivederci*, signor. *E arrivederci*, signora. *E grazie ancora*."

"*Arrivederci*, Fausto. *Grazie mille. Arrivederci!*"

They turned away. but they were not yet out of earshot when Fausto and his colleague seemed to have fallen into an angry guttural dispute. They looked back and saw the two men furiously gesticulating, Fausto waving the hand that clutched Leslie's six thousand lire. Fausto turned to see that they were watching. He waved the arm with the money at them, waved in farewell, and flashed a warm broad smile at them. They smiled back and turned away, and once more the angry voices took up their garbled duet.

As they crossed the street from the beach, walking back to their car, Leslie said, "Quite a bore, old Fausto, isn't he?"

"Do you think so?"

"And some kind of Nazi besides."

"Nonsense. He has no politics at all!"

"All that guff about German efficiency."

"I've heard Italians who positively loathe Germans praise their efficiency. They almost necessarily admire what they generally don't have."

"So?"

"And incidentally, I don't think you should have paid Fausto separately."

"But why not? He gave us a huge chunk of his day."

"I know. But he was thinking of himself as our friend and the money was somehow wrong, the wrong note on which to end."

"Listen, you know Italians—"

"Yes. And I'm sure he was getting at least half of the four thousand."

"You think so?"

"I know so. And that quarrel, I'm sure, came from the old man insisting that Fausto owed him half of the two thousand as well." Leslie was unlocking the car doors when she asked suddenly, "May I drive back?"

"Of course, if you want to."

"It hurts me the way you ride the clutch on a still very new car."

"I don't."

"Every time you shift. And you always brake before you take any curve, instead of—"

"We've been through that. Instead of letting up on the gas and accelerating on the curve."

"Yes, dear. I wish you'd learn to do it. But may I drive?"

"I said, Of course," and he gave her the keys.

She whipped off the jacket of her suit as if she were in fact putting on armor. The white gloves were gone, he noticed only now, and with them the white scarf around her head. She smiled at him and looked about twenty years old in the simple sleeveless dress that was under the jacket.

As they drove out of Passignano and up the winding highway to the point where it leveled off, he looked at her competent brown hands, the slim fingers just resting on the wheel as, expertly, she took the curves and, when she had to shift, never let her foot rest on the clutch one second beyond the necessary fraction of time. It was beautiful.

His eyes strayed up the slim unencumbered brown arms bowed to the wheel, and, thinking of her watch again, lost and retrieved so long ago, he saw with a start that it was not on her wrist now.

"Good Lord," he said, "you haven't done it again, have you? You can't have!"

"What?" she asked, without taking her eyes from the road.

"Lost your watch."

"No," she said.

"But where is it?"

"I gave it to him this time."

"You *what?*"

"I gave it to Fausto."

"In God's name, why?"

"It was little enough."

"And you didn't want me even to tip him."

"This was different. A gift."

"But what for?"

"For what he gave me."

"Which was?"

Now she hesitated. She smiled faintly. The wind was blowing her loose hair back. She had never looked prettier than in that moment. "The castle!" she said.

"The castle?"

"Yes. He was quite sweet up there, suddenly whimsical. He said, 'Signora, the castle is in fact mine, and I give it to you.' He said it very seriously."

"What nonsense!"

"No. It *is* mine now. And I'll never have to see it again to keep it." Then, as they hit a straight stretch of empty highway, she pushed the car up to fifty, sixty, sixty-five, and in a few minutes she said coolly, half question, half statement, "And you got your story?"

When he finally answered, quite listlessly, he said, "I've lost it for good," and he saw a curve coming up again in the road. The unscholarly shoe on her right foot tipped back on its high heel and the speed of the Mercedes dropped responsively. Then, at the very middle of the curve, it came down again, and the wheels clung close. Beautifully executed!

Leslie put his hand to his breast pocket, where his engagement book was. The full name was written there: Fausto Cavallare. But it might better have been Carone after all, he thought. Briefly he let himself wonder whether her watch was really in the beach bag, with her gloves and her scarf, before he concluded that it did not make any difference. Then, slumping forward a bit and ducking his head, as if he were preparing either to buck a storm or bend to a lash, he asked her, "Who's the best unpublished writer that you know?"

LUCK

*I*t was autumn in 1935. Another graduate student, Russell Barker, with whom I was sharing an apartment on Sterling Court, was standing with me on Langdon Street at the foot of the stairs that led up to the main entrance of the Student Union building. At the top of those stairs a girl in a short black dress and an elbow-length black cape and a large, floppy-brimmed, black felt hat emerged with a man named Jack Lyons, a brilliant, flabby, drunken instructor in the Department of English under whose direction, I learned later, she had written her senior thesis on Amy Lowell. Russell knew Jack well. "Who is that girl?" I asked him. He said, "Ruth Page." I said to myself, That is the girl I want to marry. But I must have said it aloud, because he said, "So does everyone."

What arrow had hit me? Something in the superb carriage? the smart costume and the shiny spike heels? the head held high and proud on the long, slim neck? the splendid walk? I had seen a dancer, a thousand years older, who worked in and out of Chicago, with the same name, Ruth Page, but I didn't know then, of course, that *my* Ruth Page, up at the top of those stairs, aged twenty-two, was also, in her less spectacular way, a dancer, any more than I knew what had hit me. But I knew.

Russell arranged our meeting. Ruth, who lived in New York, was visiting her parents in Madison and entertaining a college friend, Cate Davis, as a house guest. Cate Davis sat on a fortune, and Ruth, with characteristic irony or perversity or the generous thought that a poor graduate student such as I might well share all that money, told Russell that I was to be Cate's date and she, Ruth, his, Russell's.

Both girls wore long, white chiffon dresses, lovely visions out of the opening scene in "*Gatsby*," and we went to the Chanticleer, a restaurant outside Middleton, a little town nearby, ate such dinner as it offered, and danced.

At some point I tried to embrace Cate, but it all dissolved in hilarity on the floor of the back seat of the car that Ruth was driving.

Later I called her and she came to our apartment (Russell gone) before lunch. We had a cocktail, a dreadful Manhattan (much too much sweet vermouth), and then went on to the Union for lunch, where I (in my recollection) asked her to marry me. She says that, on the contrary, I made a long speech in which I announced that I did not believe in marriage, that I had lived all my life through a disastrous one and had no wish to risk anything like a duplication for myself, and . . . and what? I think now that Ruth's recollection is probably the accurate one. Many years later I was sent a questionnaire from some woman's periodical, *Ladies' Home Journal* or something of the sort, for an article on male attitudes toward females. The first question was "What do you most admire in women?" My answer was "Their sense of fact."

Be that as it may, when the Christmas holidays came

that year I went to New York (for the first time; during my
year in Cambridge I was too poor, or thought that I was, for
even such an unambitious excursion, Boston–New York–
Boston), checked into a fleabag across the street from
Ruth's Waverly Place apartment, and was with her constantly. We saw a lot of plays and heard a lot of music.
On Christmas Eve she took me to a party at the apartment
of her brother Robert, at 3 East Eighty-fifth Street. Robert
Page was one of those people who is a success from the
beginning: Andover, Yale, "Bones" of course, Harvard Law
School, editor of the *Law Review*, clerk to Justice Brandeis,
et cetera. When I met him he was a senior partner in the
firm of Debevoise, Plimpton, et cetera, ending with Page—
all for rhythm. Ruth, since I had seen her in the early
autumn before this wintry Christmas in New York, had
decided to give up dancing, even though she had been per-
forming quite regularly with a successful small dance group.
She had decided that she began dance too late in her life to
be anything less than magnificent, and why be anything
less? She was happy to let that talent devolve on the child
who was presently to be our daughter, Suzanne, our Suki,
who began her dance instruction at five and became a
principal dancer with George Balanchine, in whose school
she now teaches, along with those great dancers of the past,
Felia Doubrovska and Alexandra Danilova, and that fine
British teacher, Muriel Stuart, who was taught by and
danced with Anna Pavlova. Now Ruth Page was devoting
herself to a correspondence course in accounting. I think
that Robert's wife, Jerry, to whom I am devoted, liked me,
although I have no idea whether or not she approved of
my bruited marriage plan.

That Christmas party left me, straight out of Wisconsin, a bit boggle-eyed. There were not only Robert and
Jermain Page, and Jerry's two splendid, very articulate young
daughters, Janey and Annie, but also Jerry's first husband,

their father, Bill Walling, a rather flashy "man about town" type (they existed then), head of a fine printing company, and his present wife, a very smart French woman named Alicia, a buyer at Macy's, whose long fingernails were lacquered black. Ruth, who knew all these people, moved about easily with them, of course; I did not. After our evening at her brother's house, he called her and advised her to stay with her accounting.

I can understand that. The straw from my rural world must still have been sticking out of my ears, and quite sensibly if a bit stuffily, he probably hoped that some muscular new ex-Yalie would come bounding up and demand her attention. Later, I know that he had decided that Ruth's decision was in fact not unreasonable. We never had occasion to correspond, but when I was put up for the Century, he sent me a carbon of his letter (unsolicited; I didn't even know that he was a Centurian) supporting my proposers.

I wasn't worried. I taught Ruth how to square off the corners of her sheets when she made up her bed, I suggested that she lower a little the pictures hanging on her walls, and I kept saying, "Marry me!"

I got that blasted Ph.D. out of the way in June of 1936 and we were married on the following August 15.

Now, this evening, a foggy northern California evening, August 15, 1976, forty years later, we are sitting in front of a low-burning fire, only the two of us, drinking Dom Pérignon. One New York friend has told us that we are the only two people he knows neither one of whom has been divorced. Another New York friend has told us that we are the only two people she knows neither one of whom has been in analysis. This is no boast. These omissions may have been our errors. We did, though, survive. Still—Ruth is now looking speculatively at a large vase of rubrum lilies. I give her these on this day each year if we are in a place where they are available. At our garden wedding, as she came uncertainly down the steps from the piazza of her mother's house and the music of Debussy's "*La fille aux cheveux de lin*" drifted out of an open window onto the heavy midsummer air, she held in her arms a great, loose bunch of these lilies. Now, sipping champagne and then putting down her glass, looking at that forty-year reminder, she quietly, reflectively asks, "Why did you really want to marry? Because it was the thing to do?" I don't think that she has ever recognized my devotion to purest grace of body and of mind, any more than she has ever been aware that she is the total mistress of that double blessing.

I feel like crying.